DATE DUE

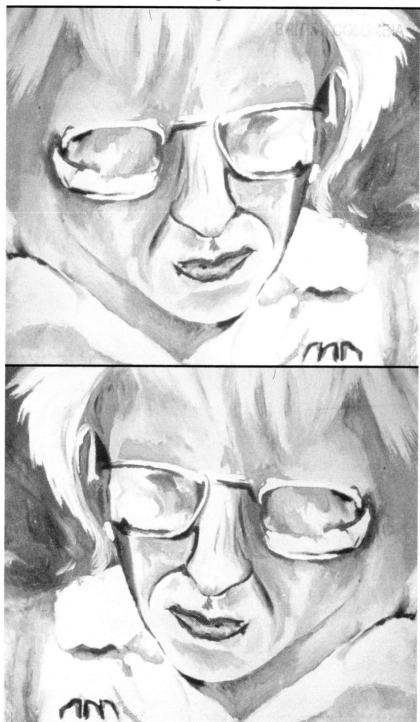

On the Road by Genni Gunn

"On the Road" was first published in *88: Best Canadian Stories*. "Rehearsal" originally appeared in *The Amaranth Review* and "Timesavers" was first published in *Black Apple*.

ISBN 0 88750 840 5 (hardcover)
ISBN 0 88750 841 3 (softcover)

Cover art by Chery Holmes
Book design by Michael Macklem

Printed in Canada

PUBLISHED IN CANADA BY OBERON PRESS

On the Road

I'm going on the road, I said to Fletch (meaning, this is a good time for a separation).

I'll write regularly, I said.

You can fly out to see me, I said.

I won't be long, I said, (packing enough things for two months).

I'll miss you, Fletch said, (but he held me as if he knew it was the last time).

On the road. The layman (non-musician) calls this "touring." We are no more touring than if we were a pack of rats infesting a village in China. Touring implies tall, air-conditioned buses with smoked windows and portable toilets; impeccable sheets and starched pillowcases; hotel rooms with a view of the sea, or the mountains, or whatever; visits to museums, art galleries and a famous/infamous dead person's home—all restored, of course, with period furniture.

We are on the road. From this vantage point, what we see is the hard grey asphalt, the vast slow movement of an orchestral forest and the frenzied rhythm of puppets in semi-darkness, whose strings we control from the stage. Or try to.

Five of us are squeezed into the van (I am the only woman) among guitars and suitcases, somebody's stereo and the front wheel of a bicycle. We're hauling a twelve-foot trailer that threatens to jack-knife at every corner. While travelling, we revert to two basic sounds: shouting or silence. I don't know which is worse. I take 222s before getting in. I've become the night driver. It is the best time—night. In the darkness, the road mingles with the forest; lines soften and I can almost forget the dreary grey of it all, dull as day-to-day existence.

I have devised a method to cope with the irrationalities to which is attached the nomenclature, "reality." I compose imaginary letters, which say all the things that escape me in those times when I most need the right words. Language is plastic, therefore not biodegradable. Thoughts are safe. I compose these letters most often during the silent night drives.

Chris keeps shifting in the front passenger seat. He always sits there at night. We've already settled into a routine. Like an old married couple. Chris is a drummer. He can't keep still—too many rhythms inside. We should be in Calgary by dawn.

Dear Fletch,

I was a gypsy travelling the taut edge of my nerves, singing to fill the caverns. You were a dark minstrel whose anguish scribbled your face. We linked arms and declared war. Our house had bunkers, sandbags all around. We were one against the world, our strengths and weaknesses carefully balanced in each other. A true illusion/delusion of equality. No-one existed outside those barriers that forced us into close scrutiny. Now I see we are mutations

too intimate
two strangers discovered.

Our love was the leaf of a coastal winter. It took two summers to wither.
Was, *Fletch*, was. *Time to move on.*

If he could hear these words,

he'd say, why? (no, he'd shout it)
he'd say, WHAT'S WRONG?
he'd say, WHAT HAVE I DONE?

This is how Fletch is. Self-centred. What have *I* done, he'd say.

Dear Fletch,
It's not something you've done at all. It is me. *I have realized:*

I'm not your mother.
I'm not your slave.
I'm not your possession.
I am.

Chris says, you want one of these? He's popping a couple. Sure. Something to keep me awake (I'm not justifying here), no appetite and my head buzzing as if a swarm of hornets are nesting in my brain.

Fletch, do you remember the nest I knocked down from the eaves above the balcony door? Sliced it open and found a perfect brain, or a condominium complex—all those nooks and crannies and floors and windows and doors. No honey, though.

It was the morning after the night you were so angry because you were late for work and couldn't get a taxi, and it was snowing outside (like it rarely does in Vancouver), and the car had no snow tires, and you didn't know, and

it's all your fault, you said;
why didn't you tell me, you said;

you must have *known* this would happen, you said (as if I'd planned it)

and then you smashed your fist into one of the nine small squares of the window in the balcony door. And a hornet flew in and bit you on the arm.

I should have laughed (I wanted to).
I should have said, you're absurd (I thought it).
I should have shouted, serves you right (and patted the hornet on the head)

but you were so *serious*. Knuckles bleeding, a welt on the upper arm, all held out to me for sympathy. And I led you like a child to the bathroom, dabbed on the alcohol (blow, blow, there, there), stuck on bandaids that lifted when you straightened your hand, and avoided looking into your eyes for fear I would collapse and laugh until I cried. Later I did (laugh) after the taxi drove you away.

I'm wired, Chris says. How much longer?
I shrug. My teeth are clenched so tight I have to speak around them. A couple of hours. Maybe three.
He pulls out a pair of sticks from behind the seat and starts drumming on his knee.
You wanna do the States? he asks.
You got paper and pen? I say.
Yeah. Sure. Alphabetical or random?
Whatever.
It's one of our pastimes. Trying to name all the US states. We always manage to miss a couple, like Oklahoma or Wyoming or Connecticut or New Hampshire. Never Hawaii or Alaska.

When we get to Calgary, we have to unload all the equipment, set it up, do a soundcheck. We're operating through sheer chemical force. Nothing natural about being up 25 hours. We all did a few lines before coming down from the hotel rooms. We're on fast-forward mode, gums desensitized, front teeth frozen, and the thoughts are racing so quickly we can only verbalize one in seven:

Would you move that…
Turn it into the…
When we get to the second set…
And the intro…
Forty-five min…
What do you mean three…
And then they said there was…

We're finished by 1 PM. I need a drink, Chris says. I gotta come down a bit.

Starting time is nine tonight. I go to my room, buzzing. Unpack. Iron all my clothes, Brush where my teeth must be. Undress. Shower. Pull on a nightgown. Lie down. Mattress lumpy and soft. I have to sleep. So tired. Unclench. Unclench.

The night-time parts, the playing—hardly worth thinking about. After a few road trips, when all the newness rubs off (not unlike a love affair) you are forever desensitized. People cease to be individuals; towns cease to have names; dates cease to exist. You are only aware of Mondays (when you set up) and Saturday nights (when you tear down and drive all night, all day, sometimes all night again). So it all comes down to first and last night (which is exactly all you ever remember of a love affair too). At least in this business, there is a paycheque on that last night. Well. Perhaps it's only the currency that differs.

Dear Fletch,
    Thanks For the Memories. Hummmm. Hummmmm. I don't know the tune. Only the title. (And besides, I can't hum in my head.) Old songs, old clichés, old lovers—who can remember them all?

Dear Fletch,
    I do love you (which is not the same as being in love). Too many implications in that one word "in": in-sincere, in-secure, in-sensitive (notice all the esses, the feminine sounds). Snakes. Snakes. Hiss. Hiss. Emossssions are feminine. Soft, supple, subtle, silly, stupid, sickly—all feminine descriptions, or effeminate ones. And now, Fletch, if you could hear this:

Stop with that feminist crap, you'd say.
You're making me a monster, you'd say (using all the male M-sounds).
You're pampered and privileged, you'd say, that's the problem (male P-sounds).
Too much time on your hands to think these thoughts, you'd say (male T-sounds).
Trouble-maker-posing-problems-that-don't-exist, you'd say (using all your maleness at once).

Well. Tough. Shut your ears if you want to. And your eyes. And your whole face. If it makes you feel better. You can't invalidate me. Not any more. Because I'm not playing.

Chris is starting to fall in love with me. God. It's only been two weeks. It usually takes a little longer. One of four men always does. This is

because we're on the road;
because he's too comfortable with me;
because I'm not his wife;
because I buy my own food;
because I don't expect anything from him;
because I'm independent;
because I listen to him without commenting; and
because he hasn't gotten me into bed.

Well. I know that once this happens, he'll expect to change all of the above, which will suddenly become threatening.

Women shouldn't travel alone, he'll say.
You shouldn't be so…friendly with men, he'll say. They'll get the wrong idea.
How could you go off like that, all afternoon, he'll say, and not tell me?
Naturally, I assumed we'd have dinner together, he'll say, especially after…
Why don't we share a room at the next place? he'll say. Everyone knows anyway.

And there would end all independence and I'd be back to where I was before I went on the road.

I can't even pretend to be falling in love with Chris. This sensation is too predictable. I used to deny the voice inside me and listen instead to a mother's words saying:

Good girls only have sex with a man they love.
He won't respect you if you do.
Play the game.
Use it to get what you want.
Sex is your best weapon. Weapon. Weep. On.

Well. Weep is something I won't do. Weeping belongs to tragic heroines or victims or silly brainless twits. If I have the need to, I cry. It has a harder, more real sound. Plastic pellets falling on corrugated iron. It's only salt and water. The worst thing for wounds.

I've only declared "I love you" twice. Once, so long ago I don't remember, and the second time to Fletch in our early days, before I knew him.

I begin to avoid Chris, to spare him all the anxiety; treat him like one of my brothers, and all that happens is he falls in love even more.

We drive at night. Saskatoon, this time. (What routing.) He wants to play States.

I'm sick of it, I say.
Oklahoma, Wyoming, Connecticut & New Hampshire, I say.
It's boring, I say.

Dear Chris,
Why the hell don't you take a downer for a change, shut your eyes and quit giving me that hurt look.

What else is there to do on the road, he says.

Life is a bore, he says.
I need adventure, he says.
I don't love my wife, he says.
You are beautiful, he says.
You are desirable, he says.
What's wrong with me? he says.

Back to that. I stare straight ahead and dig through my brain for the right phrases. The ones mothers teach their daughters to go along with the TRUTH: Men have fragile egos.

I'm already involved with someone, I lie.
I think you're very attractive (half-lie).
If there were going to be someone, it would be you (another lie).

Smile. (Fake.) There, in the dark. One side of my face cracks open. Christ, I can't feel my teeth. Everything's going to fall out all at once.

Smile, you goddam fool. It'll pass.
I can't.
Smile. Wider. Wider. Wider.

Christ. Every lie I ever told is falling out of the corners. Plastic.

I look at Chris. He smiles. Embarrassed but pleased. Well. Another lie gone direct to the muscles. He's sitting up straighter. I let him keep his hand on my thigh for a full 30 seconds before I say, get the pencil, we'll do the States. Every goddamn one of them (just to keep his fingers off my skin and his ego on the passenger side).

Dear Fletch,

I have always drifted alone in the fragile stalks of prairie wheat, lulled by the moans of farmers mourning losses. I'm settling into the knobby surface of a chenille bedspread, on an Alberta night, as stars mount hoodoos sculpted in sandstone—a Stonehenge transient as the wind's moods—windows open, enticing a shift in destiny. Above, the moon mimics the earth. I have been treading the liquid warmth of friends, the undulating wave of lovers, the inevitable epiphany of self-preservation. If only we could go on being lovers and never live together.

A mother's voice says:

> You don't mean that.
> You need a man.
> Sex is a tool, a weapon, a gun, an upper, a downer, a need, a want, a whimsical, fantastical sensation.
> You need protection.
> You need affection.
> You need LOVE.

Well. Okay. It sounds nice (the last one, I mean). But. When I look inside the pictures of love, I see spent itineraries and women/marionettes bobbing at odd angles, mouths gaped wide as frames trying to utter sound.

And now I will truly tell the truth about what happens at night and why it is not worth thinking about.

There is a stage with a carpet black & red, black & blue, black & —.

There are five of us in our stage clothes (shiny, satin, silky—all those s-sounds) to go with the lights and the illusions (like women).

There are microphones, guitars, basses, drums, sticks, organs—all the male genitalia reproduced in wood and metal—a constant erection. (The females are only passive receptacles in the walls that the males plug into.)

There is a room full of people who:

> like music, and/or
> are lonely, and/or
> need a drink, and/or
> are trying to forget themselves.

Dancing is foreplay. Watch two people dance. Hear their bodies speak. Feel the tension in the space between them, drawing them closer.

We are voyeurs and conductors; lavish orchestrators of fancies. Each set is carefully designed to bring this foreplay to a climax. Leave them breathless and pounding for an encore. Magic. Illusion.

In the daytime, we roam the streets, ordinary people. Unnoticed, unwanted, unimportant.

But what do you do for a living? they ask.
What an exciting life, they say.
You are so lucky, so talented, so free, so everything that we want, they say.

Well. So much for illusion.

On the road. Five, six weeks. My hormones are mutating. Malfunction. The asphalt grey, straight and narrow, bridges a hypnotic gulf back ten years, back to eighteen. My feet accelerate on the plank to the altar where a tall young groom awaits. My father transfers me man-to-man and I, versed in dependence, repeat the words, "honour and obey." At the motel, I shiver in a strange bed, listening to a mother's eyes. This man can only possess the flesh; he cannot read inside my head the tablets inscribed with the betrayal of women.

There, in the pretence of that moment, the first seed sprouted when his foreign body claimed sovereignty.

Dear Fletch,
   We have travelled the road together on the wings of a phoenix.
   Remember the Oregon coast, rough and turbulent as the hardening jigsaw of my convictions, clouds heavy with the sweat of industry and the cold breath of atrophied women?
   Remember a Nevada desert, arid faces eroded with desolation and the incessant sanding of the spirit?
   Remember the concrete slabs, Arizona monuments; you erecting cardboard castles tall enough to ensure death in a fall, and I masoned into the four walls, observing the world through a sliver of lemon light?
   Remember the lush green of New Mexico, communes, a social distribution. Serene faces, my emotions tie-dyed into the flowers of my skirt or

around the neck.
Remember a Colorado park of red stone, blood caked dry.
I found myself suddenly alone.

I want to be in love, I think.
I want to make love, my body says.
I want LOVE, a mother's voice shouts.

My heart's valves tighten. Function/malfunction. I spit out excess blood into Saskatchewan swamps when no-one is looking, and wear lipstick to conceal the drained smile, my pupils glazed with the opalescence of marble no man can scratch.

In my room, I lie in bed and listen to the whispers below my window; to the laughter next door; to the unoiled springs of a bed in the room above—those lonely, empty sounds of lovers battered one against the other, trying to find themselves still bleeding.

On the road. Where that cold hard surface permeates me; where I become the road, cracked but able to withstand the weight of many travellers.

When I return home, I haven't written Fletch a single letter, and all his things are gone. There is only the lingering of romantic memories, light as the whisper of air through the shattered pane of the window above the balcony door.

Rehearsal

Vince, the guitar player, sits next to me in the back seat of the van. I'm scribbling down impressions. A succinct record of the drive.

It's another road trip, only this time I'm running to, not from something. A dramatic change in perspective. Similar to going shopping with or without money in your wallet. The shops overflow with your desires when you can't afford them, and are vacant when you can.

Running from something is a collection of negatives. Not answering the phone; not asking for mail; not leaving a forwarding address; not talking to anyone. Introversion; locked doors; a virtual prisoner in the hotel room when not performing.

This trip, however, is one taken to start new things. Out of boredom. Need for change. To fall in love.

"You're lonely," Vince says, reading over my shoulder.

Sometimes just for the driving. A kind of lobotomy. All North American society is represented in the drive between Vancouver and Regina. Easy to fantasize myself into each lifestyle, but only for an impractical moment. The grass is not always greener. There's been drought. Everything's burnished brown and dusty.

Road fantasies:

Secluded log cabins
the dense woods of Golden
peaceful, remote.
I huddle in the glimmer of flames
licking the lips of a wood stove,
and read aloud
fingers entwined with those
of a dark man with no face.

Farmhouses in Lethbridge
steepled barns
red and white, gleaming in sunlight
I awaken to purple clumps of clouds
the sound of crickets,
lose myself
in the whispering of wheat stalks.

Small towns, general stores
quaint, friendly
Saskatchewan
I watch the rise of a harvest moon
an orange wafer
guarding twilight
and walk the dusty streets
etching a trail among familiar faces
where everyone knows my name.

"Face it," Vince says. "You're not one of those small-town girls."

"Women," I correct him.

"Nor are you one of those back-to-the-land *persons*."

"How do you know, anyway?" I say, annoyed, because he's right.

Enough romantic renderings. So far, all the road has yielded is a prolonged bout of existential malaise. There must be someone happy somewhere.

Blackout. We stumble off the darkness of the stage into the dressing-room. An acrid taste of reality. No Hollywood decor; no wall-to-wall mirrors framed by round makeup lights; no closets filled with sequined costumes; no easy chairs. This is a basement room, small and windowless. Against the south wall, an old couch spills matting from a hole in the armrest. Beside it leans a crooked wooden table with metal legs, covered with an array of half-empty glasses—some last night's. There are four stacking chairs—the kind one sees in a school auditorium and, of these, two are stuck together and used as one. Under the table, a pink plastic bowl overflows with red and green pellets—rat poison. This is a Rock-&-Roll dressing-room; nothing unusual about it. Often, one of the band members will leave a signature: a fork punched into the wall, a smashed lightbulb, footprints on the ceiling. On the first few road trips, I complained about these conditions until a Club Manager said, "Who do you think wrecks them?" I don't complain any more.

Our costumes hang from the thinnest horizontal tubes that line the ceiling. Lightning rods. Aqueducts. Pipelines. Intestines. Who knows? Perhaps the boiler-room of a submarine. Three changes. Already the room is dank with the smell of sweat. We can hear the rumble of bass and drums from above, and the pulsing rhythm of feet on the suspended dance floor. The guys (five of them) are on chronic complaint mode.

I don't know why they want a band, one says.

They'll dance to anything.

Where the hell are the two cases of beer?

They promised. It's in the Rider.

Stiff crowd tonight.

I take my costume and go into the bathroom. Change quickly, one foot lodged against the door. None of the locks work. Check my makeup in the small compact mirror I carry. Just who am I to be this time? The sixties set. Diana Ross. "Love Child." "Stop, In the Name of Love." "Where Did Our Love Go." Percy Sledge. "When a Man Loves a Woman." All so familiar. Unrequited love. Heartbreak. Nothing but blues. Would somebody please write a happy song? Call it "The Yellows." I could use a bit of sun. Tonight, after we pack up, we're heading east.

"You want to go out for pizza later?" Vince asks.

"What? A date?" I laugh.

"Dutch."

"Maybe."

I leave the dressing-room, walk upstairs and watch the disembodied glow of flesh under coloured lights. Eyes like headlights on a dark night. Different sizes. Dim. Bright. Low beams. High beams. There are many here, in Davy Jones' Locker. A virtual traffic jam. Medicine Hat converted to

Hawaii
leis   Christmas tinsel
tacked to the cornice round the room
the bandstand   a float
cardboard palms   real bananas
grass-skirted waitresses
bikini tops   frosted glasses
orange and pink
bamboo umbrellas bobbing amid ice
and coconut swivel sticks.

Early make-believe tacky. Perhaps it is simply a matter of perspective. The eye triggering something in the mind—a honeymoon, the colours of spring, an exotic perfume. I parallel park against a solid wall.

"Watch yourself," Vince says, suddenly at my elbow. "Some of these guys are so smooth you could spread them on toast." He winks. Moves on.

He's becoming increasingly possessive about me. Protective. I don't mind, as long as we remain friends. On the road, we are a family. Bicker and shout. Comfort and cry. Sometimes, we fall in love out of loneliness. Sometimes, we fall in love with

loneliness. A one-way mirror to seal the turmoil. For months now, my road's been straight and narrow. No stunt driving here. "Better to play it safe," I tell the guys who incorrectly interpret this cliché only in terms of sex.

Detached, I watch the mating rituals on the dance floor. Far from being the centre of things, performers are always on the perimeters. Looking in. Misfits. Across the room, a man leans against the opposite wall, mimicking me. His smile tunnels through the shifting crowd and I recognize not him, but his eyes, my eyes.

The stranger triggers a fantasy:

an ebony night   a highway
oncoming car   high beams
I'm powerless   lured
into the hypnotic glare
blind to the thin white line
   between us
a suicidal impulse to melt
into the amber brilliance
Icarus abducted by the sun.

The real danger is that loneliness creates its own perspective. Hysterical desire. And suddenly an ordinary man becomes *Apollo;* a trivial conversation takes on metaphysical properties; and a sexual encounter is glorified into *Endless Love.*

I've stumbled into illusion on the road before. Same circumstances. Different stranger. Six weeks. And when the canonization was complete, I took him home with me, only to watch him metamorphose into a monstrous pink elephant. Took me weeks to get rid of him. Paul Simon said there are "fifty ways to leave your lover." But this was before that song.

"Two minutes." Vince holds up a victory sign, braking my stare.
I lurch forward, knees weak.

20

"Hey, easy. Did I scare you?" He steadies me, hands light on my shoulders.

I nod. "I'm okay."

"Scratch the second half of the encore. This crowd's too straight."

We rehearsed choreography all afternoon. Hours of practice to make it look spontaneous. It's why we do mostly one-nighters.

Those who see us a second time, realize how programmed we are. Everything is rehearsed, including the encore, including the guitar player's final leap into the audience when he must land on the imaginary X, prearranged, so the follow spot can capture his final frenzy.

On stage. Later. The music blares. From this side, it is difficult to call this music. Cymbals and bass create a cacophony of overtones. I have to plug one ear with my finger to hear myself sing. On the front side of the stage, the speakers project a balanced sound, thanks to the mixing board and the sound-man at the back of the room.

Even the lights are programmed, synched to the bass drum's heartbeat. Sequenced. Green. Red. Blue. Amber. The front pods and follow spots are operated by the light-man who squats in a small cage near the ceiling.

I lean over the edge of the stage and see the stranger approach. Warning bells ring in my head, synchronized to the flashing signals of a railway crossing, of the sequencing. I know this is ridiculous. Impossible. There's no way. But why be rational? Perhaps it's worth venturing. Even if it is only illusion. Perhaps illusion is just another word for need. He is dancing at the edge of the stage, so close, I can almost touch him.

"Take a solo, Vince," I say, stepping back into another night,

a railway crossing
moving steel
feet grinding fear
into the brake
into the clutch

shake the gearshift   four five times
neutral   yet   ensnared
the handbrake taut   seduced
by the solenoid of destruction
ignition off   and still
cowardice ploughs rhythmic furrows
into the heart.

Vince leans into me from the side. Whispers, "Watch it."
Sometimes, we fall in love out of danger. Sometimes, we fall in love with
danger. I do a crazy dance without moving my feet and count, for no reason, I count because it's better than looking at the space beneath each railcar, the space that appears large enough to go under if I could only do it fast enough to miss the wheels at either side.
The real danger is the chatter of eyes. Difficult to silence. My eyes scream vulnerability in the split of a second.
Last song. We don't do an encore and as we step off the darkened stage, I whisper, "Put your arm around me, Vince."
In the dressing-room, I change into streetclothes, pack my costumes into the trunk and check the bathroom to see that I've left nothing behind. There is at least an hour's wait until the club can be cleared so we can pack our equipment. I linger for a decent interval (playing games already), then abandon the safety of the dressing-room.
The stranger is waiting. Red lights begin to flash back and forth—his eyes programmed to a train signal. I tell myself, don't be ridiculous, he hasn't tried to talk to you, you don't know his name, he might never come over and talk to you, so why worry? I fantasize

a romance   remote
ambiguous   forgetting/recalling reason
the road a paradox
delicious anxiety   near misses

only in horseshoes
and shotguns

Vince, on my left. "Is something wrong?"

I shake my head. "No, nothing."

The scent of aftershave. Aphrodisiac. My stomach turns to knots. I stare across the room at the stranger. He reads my eyes.

Vince watches me watching him watching me.

I force myself to focus on a Hawaiian print nearby. A shirt, blue background, splashed with orange and yellow flowers. Wrinkled. Rayon. I stare intently, smelling the scent of those flowers—magnolia, ginger, I don't know—but it doesn't matter because I'm rehearsing lines.

Perhaps he'll ask, "Do you want a drink?"

Thing is, I don't drink, but I won't say that, because if I do, he'll think I'm putting him off, which is exactly what I'm trying to do but I don't want *him* to know that. So I try to calm myself (don't be ridiculous), and stare at my shoes until my eyelids ache from the force. When I look up, he is walking toward me, and the warning bells are now synchronized to my heartbeat. His eyes are

glittering steel orbs
on black asphalt
in my lane

I mumble, "Excuse me," and swerve to avoid him, pulling in too close to Vince, violating his space. He does not step back. We are inches apart. I am startled by this unexpected intimacy and reverse quickly.

"Don't worry," I say to him. "I can take care of myself."

Vince pauses, shrugs, moves on. He understands conventions. Sometimes, we fall in love by accident. Sometimes, we fall in love with

accidents. Across the room, the stranger too has swerved and braked. I *am* being ridiculous, he wasn't coming toward me. I've imagined everything. I laugh a jerky sound, to settle the sensation in my stomach, which is there on nights when I drive alone. A winter storm. How often I have fingered the headlight switch, wanting to press it in and see the road and the snow in the moonlight.

I practice

in my head   darkness
memorize the space
          between
my fingers   the dash
a straight stretch   push in the switch
eyes blind with night
inhaled breath   trembling hands
the moon explodes
white incandescent
mantle of snow
no sides   no edges

Christ. Who am I kidding? I *need* boundaries. Quickly, I pull the switch. I am still on the road. Nothing's happened. Adrenalin flows to the heart.

Switch to cruise control. But what I'm thinking is, why doesn't he come and talk to me? And, please don't let him come and talk to me. I know exactly what will happen.

"Would you like to dance?" he'll say.
    And I'll make excuses, "I don't dance."
    "There's a first time for everything."
    I'll say I like to dance but I'm self-conscious.
    "There's no reason to be self-conscious."
    I'll have to explain that I feel people are staring at me when I dance, because they've seen me on stage.
    And he'll say, "We'll, you're not on stage now."
    And how can I argue with that?

I *can* argue with that. I plan very carefully; think things out before they happen; rehearse lines for all scenes—making sure I have a script ready—because that's the only way it'll sound spontaneous.

I look across the room again but he's still parked. Traffic moves around us. A blur of colours. My eyes hurt. Where's Vince when I need him? I'm afraid I might begin to do those familiar things I do so well. Like walking past him to the bar when I already have a drink. Brush arms and maybe he'll stop me and introduce himself holding his hand out. I think this because of his eyes, and my eyes that threaten to close the gaps. I won't look at him again. I'll leave now.

Then suddenly, he's at my elbow asking, "Would you care to dance?" and I feel stupid saying no, and having to explain, I've already done that in my head. I nod instead, and wonder how his arms will feel around me and what I should say to keep a space between us. He leads me to the dance floor and the song is a fast number and all that rehearsing and wondering is for nothing.

The song is almost over. I look at him, my hands steady on the steering-wheel. He smiles and I smile back, wondering, what does he think this means? I brake my smile and watch the blinking lights. The music begins. I must count. I move my feet hard against the pedals. If we continue to dance all night, soon we'll be leaning close to each other to talk. And we'll start saying silly things, while being very aware of each other's ears and how close our mouths are. Then later, in the darkness, we'll say, "I've never felt like this before," and "This has never happened to me," yet we'll be lying because how else would we know how this feels, and how would I know this is the way it's going to be?

Vince waves me down from across the room. He draws his finger across his throat. I shake my head. Sometimes, we fall in love out of fear. Sometimes, we fall in love with

fear. The stranger's eyes advance. Too close. My feet move alone to the music's beat, as if I'm really frozen and doing a dance step to get the circulation back. Rehearse. Concentrate.

He says, "Can I get you a drink?" and I answer, "Thank you," although I've rehearsed it otherwise, and he leaves me standing there on the shoulder, near several people.

I blink once, twice, and suddenly his lights grow dimmer, distant. I've pushed in the switch and the room is white, cold with snow, no lines to guide me, no boundaries, and I'm frightened because I've forgotten where the switch is although I've rehearsed it in my head a thousand times. Keep straight, move out right now, it's not such a long way to the door.

In the dressing-room, later, Vince says, "You can come out now. He's gone."

"Thanks."

He stands in the doorway and when I gently push him through to get by, he says, "I'm mad about you," sounding strangely familiar.

I don't know whether to laugh hysterically or make love to him right there in the doorway.

Slowly, he steps into my rehearsal, completing the fall.

Private Li(v)es

After a turbulent relationship, the ending is mundane. Max and I have not even discussed it. I come home one night to an empty closet and a note that says, "Go and see Allie."

Actually, it's not night, it's early morning. 5.36 to be precise. After the gig, two band members and I went to an after-hours club called "Jonathans," a gay bar without a liquor licence (no problem though, if you know how to ask). We go there most nights. Max has never complained. He's a musician too (between gigs right now), and knows the scene.

The point is, I'm now sitting in my apartment (ours for a time, (is this a Freudian slip?)) and nothing's changed. The only disconcerting fact here, is that I feel nothing. This catapults me into a brief period of guilt (and I mean miniscule, not being too good at guilt), followed by a questioning period. Why am I *not* upset? Surely I must feel something. Have I ever felt anything? Are emotions no more than projections of needs and wants? Are needs and wants fabrications of the mind?

I make a cup of coffee, swallow two 222s and take stock: I am 25 years old and have spent the last seven years equally divided among three men. At this rate it'll take another 21 to get me through to 75 or death. And I don't mean casual encounters here. No. I mean two-and-a-third years per man, four major upheavals a decade, constant adjustment, falling in and out of love so often, I should have broken every bone in my body.

I tiptoe down the hall and knock on Allie's door. It takes her three minutes to open it a crack and peer out through half-shut eyes.

"It's me," I say. "Let me in."

She shuts the door, unlatches the safety chain, then opens it. I follow her in. She is naked and searching for her dressing-gown.

"What the hell time is it?" she says.

"Around six."

"Fuck," she says. "Normal people are getting up right now and you haven't even been to bed." She abandons her search for the dressing-gown, and puts on instead an old shirt that she deftly extracts from between two cushions of the couch.

"I waited up till 2.30," she says.

"When did he leave?"

"9.30, ten. I don't know." She pauses. "Are you upset? You don't look upset."

"Na," I say. "It's been coming a long time. It was just a matter of who would leave and when."

"Let me make some coffee," Allie says. "I'm not up to this."

She's been my best friend for five years. I've always told her everything. Well, this is not entirely true. There is the affair I had with her husband when I was in-between men for five minutes, but that was after they split up and before Allie and I became friends.

Allie's very perceptive, which is why she's not acting terribly sympathetic. But I know that if I were hurting, she'd be there for me.

Because Max and I have been leading separate lives together for the past six months, the adjustment to single life is negligible. I still come and go as I please, sleep and eat whenever I want, and justify none of my actions. How did we become like this? We must have been in love once.

Allie thinks my problem is that I have an unnatural need to define sexual attraction in terms of love. But this is because she only knows about the men I've lived with here. What she doesn't know about are the in-betweens—those nights at the end of a gig that sometimes end in a strange bed, the extension of an illusion. Performance can do this. An actress staying in character long after the curtains fall. I'm good at illusions; men always want an encore. But I'm a realist. And love is no more than a chemical imbalance. Like taking so much niacin, your skin turns beet red and you find yourself examining forgotten parts of your body, surprised to discover blood vessels pumping underneath the surface. Chemical imbalance. Like doing coke for two days and nights and eating only three apples. So I say to myself, take it easy, take a cold shower, take a good look at one of those photo albums lined up on the shelf in two-and-a-third-year installments. There's enough caustic substance in there to stabilize your chemical imbalance.

After four days, the phone rings and it's Max and he says, "I really miss you," and, "Can we talk this over?"

And I don't answer right away because we've never talked it over, though I might have wanted to before I heard his voice, but now I know there's no point, because, like it or not, the sound of his words produces only a deep weariness.

It doesn't take long for news of our split to circulate. Both Max and I are fairly high-profile in the music business. Music Business. An oxymoron. The music industry does not function on any level like a business. Who invents these terms? Military Intelligence. Amicable Divorce. Within two weeks, the male counterparts of three couples we know very well either call me or come to see me. They have obviously been talking to Max, who, in the short time we've been apart, has managed to forget all the apathy between us. These three men, all married, all Max's very good friends, come as solicitors, mediators in a dispute that never happened. What is most surprising, is the unmasked undercurrent of flirtation. It suddenly occurs to me how fragile marriage really is, and how difficult it is to tell what's really happening between two people. Of course, I choose to ignore the symptoms of all these threadbare relationships, just as I deliberately pretend to misunderstand the intent of these men's concern.

"All things considered," I tell Allie, "this is it. I am going to stay single for as long as I live."

"Sure," she says.

"I mean it, Allie."

"Let me get this in historical perspective," she says. "Since you left home, just exactly how many *days* have you spent living on your own?"

I sigh. "The point is, I'm going to do it now."

"Maybe," she says. "But don't expect me to hold my breath."

My mother was 31 when I was born—late, for those days. She has all the characteristics of the perfect fifties woman. Married at twenty, deceitful and efficient. She pulls my father along on a thin chain of manipulations; charms men with smiles and gentle words; views other women with a certain amount of suspicion and can't understand why I don't. So, when I tell her about Max, she's clearly disappointed in me, and makes a heroic gesture to blame herself.

"I should have put my foot down long ago," she says. "I've failed you."

"This has nothing to do with you, Mother. I'm old enough to fail myself."

"I should have taught you better," she says, ignoring me.

"Perhaps the problem is that you taught me too well."

As long as I can remember, Mother has indoctrinated me into my role as woman. The ultimate performance. She has always acknowledged equality of the sexes in every facet of life except love. In the latter, she has endeavoured to teach me an intricate grid system of treachery and entrapment of men. These are the Cardinal Rules:

1. Flattery (deserved or not)
2. Weakness (don't lift anything heavier than a book. It'll make him feel stronger).
3. Withholding sex, followed (after a suitable time) by submission. (Never be the first to begin foreplay. It might make him impotent.)
4. Intellectual servitude (if you know more than he does, don't say so).

I can't fault her the rules. I have absolute proof they work.

Allie says, "I can't believe you've held out for two whole weeks. So much for the single free life."

"It's just a date. Nothing's going to happen." We are both in my bathroom, sitting at the edge of the tub, lacquering our toenails into scarlet moons. There's a queasy feeling in my stomach, although I try to pretend otherwise. In the medicine cabinet, two bottles of antacid tablets defy all pretense. Bland proof of my body's revenge. Chemical imbalance. I fight my private lies with foreign substances.

The man I'm going out with has been a casual friend for over a year. Last week he came into the club and, through my new perspective as a single woman, I rediscovered him as a stranger. New camera angle; new lens. This is what attraction does. Chemical imbalance. It can turn the closest of friends into adversaries.

"So, how long has this been going on?" Allie asks.

"Nothing's been going on," I say, irritated. "You know Peter."

"Yeah. I know Peter," she says. "I know him well enough to know he's not your type."

I look at her curiously. "So, what exactly is my type?"

"You're looking for a nice, safe long-term," she says. "Peter sees the same woman twice only if the second time is an accident."

"It's only dinner," I say, wondering what Allie would think if she really knew the truth about me. "Nothing's going to happen."

Peter takes me to Chateau Madrid where waiters wear cummerbunds (Indian origin, not Spanish), and three rotund Mexican-Canadians strum badly tuned guitars at our table until Peter palms them a fiver. I wonder if this will only insure their return after the second course. Peter has been here before, he tells me. Often. I think he's trying to impress me. He is the lawyer who handled Allie's inheritance when her father died last year. Allie is probably right about types. I have an aversion to people who try to impress me, and have always preferred a man with an unpredictable disposition—a quality/detriment that I'm certain Peter does not have.

During dinner, I hear myself exercise the first of the Cardinal Rules. I admire his clothing and his eyes, which are blue or green, depending on which section of his two-tone sweater I focus on. He returns the compliments, and I wonder if his mother is like mine. It takes all my concentration to suppress the awkward, nervous tension that tightens in my stomach like a fist. Despite Peter's frown, I refuse Sangria, order and gulp four Margueritas, none of which help. My face, however, I'm quite certain, does not reflect the conflict taking place in my body; nor do my words. Private lies and public performances. Every few moments, Peter twirls the signet ring on his second finger, left hand. It's difficult to redefine a relationship after a year.

A little past midnight, when there is absolutely nothing else we can eat or drink to extend the dinner, he says, rather abruptly, "This is really awkward. Do you want to come to my place?"

Allie was right. Cardinal Rule 3. I make a joke of it, and say, "What for?"

He laughs, embarrassed, I think, then, "No pressure."

Later, I drag Allie out of bed. "Just to prove you wrong," I say.

She says, "He hasn't asked you out for a second date yet."

The first part of Cardinal Rule 3, although unintentional, is working against me when it comes to Max. I'm receiving daily phone calls on my answering machine, love letters in the mail and one delivery of flowers of the most pretentious proportions.

Two weeks pass and Peter does not call. Our gig falls through and I'm faced with a weekend at home alone. I shop Friday night until the Mall closes, then go home empty-handed and depressed. Check the answering machine, but there are no messages. I make dinner, then eat it in front of the TV, through the six o'clock news taped on the VCR, through the *New Newlywed Game,* embarrassed and fascinated with the personal details these couples are willing, no, anxious, to disclose to the rest of the world. Marriage and intimacy reduced to multiple choice.

During the last commercial, before the couple wins the prize especially selected for them, I dump the dishes in the sink and go to the study. Pick up the telephone receiver to make sure there is a dialtone. Place it back in its cradle. Fight the urge to go to Allie's and ask her to dial my number, to see if the phone is working. I resettle in front of the TV and flick channels with the changer, watching nothing, watching everything.

When I'm not working, the evenings are the hardest since Max left. There seems to be so much time and nothing to fill it with. Max was a full-time job. We may have fought, but it was better than the emptiness now.

At 9.30, I phone his new number. No reply. Not even his answering machine. Every half hour, in the commercial between programs, I phone Max. I'm not sure what I'll say if he answers, or even why I'm calling. At 11.30, his machine clicks in, but I don't leave a message.

The next day, I phone one of Max's friends, swear him to secrecy, then tell him I miss Max. Two hours later, a singing telegram arrives at my door: a man wearing a cast, singing "Since I Fell For You." All three verses. Seduced by the romanticism, the humour, the success of my own manipulation, and the lack of Peter's second phone call, I agree to see Max.

"You're copping out," Allie says. "You said you were going to stay single."

"Max and I had some very good times," I say, defensively.

"Exactly. 'Had' is the operative word."

I ask Max to meet me in the late afternoon, at the Art Gallery where spacious rooms overflow with beauty, where emotions are exhibited without shame. The apartment holds too many memories, intrinsically linked to the pattern of my life with men. There is the evidence of all three here, different, yet so similar, it's easy to confuse one with the other; three bedspreads, though the bed was always mine.

We met, foreign powers in a common market; words the currency of expression. We bartered, bought, sold, invested, amalgamated, bribed, speculated, negotiated, overbid. Love reduced to the politics of power, complete with deceptions, misconceptions, suspicion and finally, the coining of a new acerbic jargon.

In the first year with Max, with Bill, with Charles, disputes always ended in bed; in hand-to-hand combat; in the sensual pleasure that renders amnesia, the body's language more dominant than the mother tongue.

In the second year, slowly, our entwined limbs began a writhing dance of serpents avoiding the harshness of light. The bed, a pit, and sheets concealed within their folds unrealized dreams, unrealistic expectations, the sudden discovery that no amount of heat from our bodies could kindle cold words. We grew thicker skins. Called them maturity and wisdom. At night, we lay on separate sides, watching the husks of our former selves form an impregnable barrier between us.

Little by little, even words were silenced. We learned a new language of gestures, subtitles. Each wound received translated to a given one. The husk pile grew so tall, we could no longer see each other.

Then, the first cadence, and with it, gestures stopped. The acceptance of the paradox: foreign beings, sharing nakedness.

All that remained through the next four months was a false cadence, an awaiting for one to translate our common bond of isolation into the language of departure.

I walk into the Art Gallery ten minutes late, and don't look for Max. Perhaps an unconscious need to rediscover him in the pleasure of surprise that occurs when you turn a corner and see a familiar painting as totally new.

When we are face-to-face, I sense the awkwardness of what has not passed between us.

"You look wonderful," he says, taking my hand. We are standing in the middle of a forest. Emily Carr. The burnished landscapes exude the odour of mulch. Beneath the green foreground, the earth is alive with decay. An illusion, perhaps, captured in time, as brief and intangible as saying "I love you" for the first time.

When I don't reply, Max releases my hand. "Let's get out of here." His palm, now pressed into the small of my back, prods another time. We are standing at the end of a trail, at the edge of a creek bank. A log has been felled to act as a bridge, and hovers twenty feet above the fast-flowing water. Max is urging me across. "Go on. You can do it. It's no more than five, six steps."

I hold back, press myself against his palm, mesmerized by the churning eddies—evergreens distorted, a twirling reflection of branches, witches stirring a cauldron.

"Just don't look down," Max says. "Stare at the log. You can walk a straight line. You can do it." He prods me hard enough to force my right foot onto the log.

Instinctively, I grab his arm for balance; stare down at what appears as a thin wire suspended hundreds of feet above a black mouth. "I can't, Max." Leg muscles tense, body rigid.

"Oh, for Christ's sakes! Look, it's easy." He pulls me back on solid ground and steps lightly across. Once, twice, three, four times. An acrobat, repeating, "Nothing to it." Then he sits on the opposite bank and taunts me, shouting above the rushing of the water. But I do not budge. Tired of this, he gets up and disappears down the trail into the thick forest.

I continue to sit on my side of the creek. Too frightened to go either forward or back, I pass the time counting the number of twigs that spin in the vortex of the river. I count sixteen; perhaps an hour passes; perhaps more or less.

I see Max before I hear him. He comes toward me, face set stubborn, and hauls me up. Then, he pulls me onto the log. I struggle, suddenly unsure as to his intentions. After three steps, I stumble, and Max lets go of my hand. I crouch on the log, arms tight around it.

"Damn you," he says, and crosses to the other side, leaving me stranded.

Slowly, I inch backwards, straddling the log, until I reach the bank. Here, I sit on the ground and cry. Max remains on the opposite bank until every last sob has stopped. Then, he skips across the log and begins the walk home, with neither a backward glance, nor a word.

"I don't want to go to a restaurant," Max says. "I want to talk to you. Let's get some Chinese take-out and go home."

"It's not your home any more, Max," I say, knowing this will hurt him, wanting to hurt him.

At the Chinese take-out, we disagree over the order and Max, instead of compromising, buys everything he wants and everything I want. We leave the restaurant with $40 worth of Chinese food eight people couldn't eat.

In the apartment, we face each other across the table and Max delivers a monologue. "I couldn't take it any more. The house a total mess, and you out all night. When was the last time you cooked a meal?"

"Max, you've been out of work for a while. Why couldn't you do some of those things?" As I say this, I know I'm breaking a Cardinal Rule my mother would consider too sacred to require a mention. Like "Do Not Kill."

"There. That's the whole problem," he says. "You've changed. When I met you, you wouldn't have said something like that. You wouldn't have been so—"

"Honest, perhaps? You're right, I have changed. But so have you. It's natural. Maybe we've just changed at different rates."

"Or into different people," he says. "I don't know you any more."

I push my food around my plate. No longer hungry. The colours are all too vivid. Nauseating. I push my chair away from the table and go into the bedroom to lie down. Old habits die hard. Max follows me in, and lies beside me.

We make love, but it is not love; a wooden, desperate performance. There is no tenderness between us. No pleasure. Max rolls onto his back; we lie silent, each in our own thoughts.

Then, he says, "I'm sorry," and I wonder for what. For leaving? For coming back? For the dull emptiness he too must feel, this stranger so near and so apart from me.

"Please go." I shut my eyes and listen to the rustle of his clothes. The corduroy pants, the fly, the satin lining of his jacket sleeves. Before he leaves, he kisses my eyelids, gentle as two drops of rain.

When he is gone, I turn on the News, take a Valium, lie on the couch, and dream wide-awake, and for a moment, anything is possible. We could begin again, if only we could invent one dictionary to define our needs. Even the TV appreciates paradox and the sub-

36

jectivity of definition. In one hemisphere, a city curses the aftermath of rain; while in another, a village prays for its return.

Timesavers

The last week of a three-month tour. Anxieties begin to surface. Predictable. Difficult to mistake.

On stage. Third set (classic old rockers), sixth song. "Gimme Some Lovin' " by Spencer Davis. One of my favourites. The intro: a primal rhythm of five beats pounded in succession, then the bassdrum kicks a reply, guttural as breath escaping a strangled throat. It never fails to evoke a pelvic thrust, involuntary as the hanged man's ejaculation. Music is a language stronger than reason.

We reach the chorus and when I sing, "Gimme Some Lovin'," Shane omits his harmony (the third), so that the echo of my words resonates in hollow perfect fifths, rendering the blues refrain as a Gregorian chant.

Christ. I look at him and mouth the words, "Sing your fucking harmony."

Shane turns away, but only after he is absolutely certain that I know that he is deliberately ignoring me.

Anxieties. Like when it's time for his guitar solo. Shane is an innovative musician. It's what is most attractive about him. Perhaps the only thing. He breathes solos. Tonight, however, he strums rhythmic chord patterns and stares straight ahead at a fixed point a foot above the audience, a simulated bored expression on his face. It takes three or four bars before the keyboard player covers for him, improvises a synthesizer solo when, clearly, the part is designed for guitar.

Anxieties. Both his and mine. Our time is over. In three days we'll be home. He is my sister's fiancé.

On a break. I pass the time standing at a table near the bar. Chat inanely.

Shane stands at the edge of the stage. Scowls at me. When he sees me looking, he nods toward the doorway. I shake my head, then smile at the man closest to me. Anxieties. A primal form of communication.

Shane and I came together because of familiarity and loneliness. A few weeks of travel and several thousand strangers after you leave home, it is natural (if not necessary) to fabricate human contact. Not as a need for love, but as a rebellion against the anonymity of being a public person. And a bandmember is a real timesaver. An illusion of intimacy. The tricky parts are when one or the other forgets it's illusion.

By the last set of the last night, I know there'll be a showdown. Shane has refused to sing any of his songs; I've had to repeat three of mine to cover the time. Finally the last cymbal crash. I linger at the bar, chat with customers, gulp two scotches. I'm still in the club three-quarters of an hour later, when the audience begins to spill out the doors encouraged by the bouncers' cries, "Hotel/Motel time, folks. Everybody out."

I get in the elevator and go up to the room. Shane opens the door before I can insert my duplicate key. He's been listening for the sound of my heels in the hall. Dog's ears perked for a familiar car horn.

"Don't make this any harder," I say.

"I don't want you talking to people." He grabs my arm, nails digging.

"I'll talk to whomever I please."

"No you won't."

"You're hurting me." I push against him, but he holds tighter.

A door opens across the hall. The drummer. "What's going on?"

Shane stares, uncertain. Then he releases my arm. "Damn bitch!" He slams the door.

I sigh, shrug at the drummer and walk down the hall to my own room. Many of my clothes are in Shane's room; I've been spending more time there than in mine. But I do have my bass guitar with me. A sanity mechanism. I play it for hours each day, without plugging it in. No sound, just the slap of my fingers against the fretboard.

I lie on the bed and stare at the concrete white walls, the screwed-down lamps, the pen and paper-pad on the particle-board desk. A semblance of domesticity. Ironic that a passion for music would usher me into such sterility.

Off the road for a week. A much-needed rest. The band drops me off in front of the apartment I share with my sister, Tara.

I go up, wary, but she's not home. She works shifts. I unpack slowly, then lie on the couch and stare at the ceiling.

Tara arrives within the hour. Shane must have called her. She hugs me, and begins to shed her clothes on the way to the bathroom. I hear the water begin to run, then splashes.

"Selene?" she calls. "Are you coming?"

Ever since Tara reached her mid-teens, the two of us have used the bathroom as a confessional. It began as a natural refuge from Mother. I, coming home between gigs, would listen to Tara's current heartbreak, offer biased advice on everything, answer questions and tell humorous stories (often embellished) about my lovers. One of us would be in the bath; the other sitting on the lip, feet immersed to mid-calf. To baffle our voices, we kept the water running through it all (no stopper, one of us pushed her heel in the drain whenever the level got too low). When we suspected Mother was eavesdropping, we spoke loudly of clothes and shopping, giggling hysterically, making lewd gestures with our fingers and tongues. Even after Tara left home, we continued this ritual. It seems natural, if somewhat perverse, for us to shed our clothes and hop in a bath when we want to divulge secrets.

"Selene?" she calls again.

I walk into the bathroom and sit, fully clothed, on the edge of the tub.

"Come on," she says. "Strip. It's been three months. Tell all." She smiles, childlike and excited.

I watch her; in my mind, making deals with God: please, don't let her know. I'll do anything. I can't bear for her to know.

"Not much to tell," I say.

"You? I don't believe it for a minute." She sits up in the tub, making room for my feet. "Come on."

"I'm not in the mood," I say, and leave.

"Selene?" she calls out after me.

Later, I go in and take a shower; keep the door locked. Tara knocks, but I pretend not to hear.

Shane comes to pick her up in late afternoon. Tara has tried on everything she owns, washed and dried her hair twice, gone and bought new lace panties, and still she's not ready. I stay with her in the bedroom. When she's finally satisfied with her appearance, she pulls me out into the living-room. I stand as far away from Shane as possible. Tara puts on her coat and opens the door.

"Why don't you come with us, Selene?" Shane says.

Tara looks from Shane to me, surprised.

"Na," I say. "You guys want to be alone. Besides, I've got a date," I lie.

"With whom?" Shane asks.

"Some guy."

"How'd you have time to meet some guy?" Shane says. "You've

hardly been home an afternoon."

"Hey," Tara says, "what's this? The third degree? Selene's old enough to take care of herself."

Shane glares at me, then shrugs. "You're right. She is."

Passion and intensity. What else could possibly motivate a human being through the drudgery of existence? Imagine your life as a straight line. A horizon dropping into the ocean. "Life's a bitch and then you die," someone said. Great. Why bother with the bitch part?

The silence haunts me; an unusual sound. It's Friday night; the clubs are full. In my head, echoes: singles, out hunting in meat-markets, the musk of sex confused with the smell of blood. Shoot now; pay later.

The problem with passion and intensity is that they require an enormous amount of time and energy. Something I sorely lack. I spend 48 weeks a year in as many cities. Work six nights a week. The one day off is a tedious drive between gigs, often between provinces. The remaining four weeks serve as rest-stops every three months. Often I spend this time rehearsing with a new band. Imagine five musicians on the road—like solitary confinement. The survival statistics are dismal. If I'm lucky, and find myself home and not rehearsing, I have no energy for even a casual affair. This is the glorious, glamorous life of a musician. Existence, wrought with recurring bouts of existential angst, like malaria. I recover, though. Lots of practise.

I've been staring at the TV, sound turned off. I'm used to this; I watch live serials from the stage every night. Rarely listen to the soundtrack. I can accurately predict who'll walk out with whom, without hearing the drivel in between. A real timesaver.

Strange, the limits of time. In astronomy, time is a variable, n suspended as a power: 10 to the power of n. A rhyme. An abstract idea. Infinite. In history, time is a chronology, neatly dissected by Christianity. BC/AD. No Future. In humans, time is a small range of life expectancy. Finite. "He died of old age, you know." Only for a human. A star dies after 23 million years on earth.

Perhaps the last half of this century will be measured in second increments. If I were to buy a new bass tomorrow, it would be obsolete before my VISA card could be validated. This is the reason I don't own a microwave. I'm waiting for someone to invent a way to cook food inside the packing bags as I drive home from the grocery store. A microtrunkwave. Plug it into the cigarette lighter. A real timesaver.

I find the remote, and tap the channel changer till it reaches 17 (an even pressure would do it automatically, but much slower). The familiar graphic begins on the vertical-split screen. Cartoon figures of men on one side, women on the other, as if on a film reel. Both sides spin in opposite directions. When they stop, animation begins and two things can happen: the cartoon couple can kiss or quarrel. TV imitating life, and vice-versa.

The phone rings and the answering machine kicks in. Shane. "I know you're there, Selene. Pick up the damn phone." He's left similar messages ten, twelve times a day all week, when he knows Tara is at work. I rewind the tape often, my privacy insured by the marvels of technology. The intercom downstairs is connected to the phone. No one gets past the answering machine. I imagine Shane standing in the dark below, perhaps staring up twelve storeys at the light in the apartment.

Shane's been replaced by a new guitar player. One of us had to go. And a female bass player's too big a draw. We rehearsed until yesterday.

The show is called, "The Love Connection," though what it has to do with love or connection is beyond any conjecture. I watch episodes whenever I'm home, for no other reason than to reassure myself that I have not reached this level of desperation. The contestants are ordinary people, with such time constraints, they resort to choosing partners from videos. One date only. Then they come on the show to deliver the verdict. There's only one way to better this: two screens facing, switch on the videos and skip the date. Now this would be a real timesaver.

They come to Show and Tell, every smutty detail, every insult, every look, touch, sound, smell and feel. Rarely do couples connect. This is a peep show. Nothing is sacred. A public display of

43

idiosyncracies, personal hygiene, embarrassing moments, whatever:

—The first thing I noticed was his receding hairline.

—And after dinner, she used a toothpick at the table.

—And he spoke so loud, everyone was looking at us.

—Well, I said to myself, I sure hope I don't meet any of my friends.

—And he kept telling me about all the girls he'd slept with.

Primitive cultures used stones; here the audience presses buttons in the side of the armrests. I vote out loud in front of the TV. Don't pick number three, I say, he's a jerk.

The phone rings again, as if to mock me. I should talk. I'm an expert at choosing my men. Shallow or married.

"Selene. I've got to talk to you. It's very important."

I switch off the volume on the answering machine.

The premise of the show is this: a wo/man comes out and as s/he stands smiling, a voice-over informs the homeviewers and the studio audience as to the person's vital statistics (in this case: name, age, occupation and marital status, in that order of importance). This appears on the side of the screen with the clickety-click of each letter—a sound borrowed from old reruns of the Million Dollar Wo/Man. Techumans.

After the vital statistics, come one or two sentences of introduction in the person's own words (while s/he continues to smile for the camera). To illustrate character.

—She says she loves a man who works out every day and makes at least $40,000 a year.

—This young man says he's interested in an intelligent woman because an intelligent woman can pretend to be dumb and still be intelligent.

The studio audience votes. *They* know. This is the age of polls. Democracy and all that. Their choice is always better than the individual's.

I watch the show for the same reason people ask me why I'm not married. They get a vicarious pleasure in knowing someone has screwed up worse than they have.

44

"But why?" they say. "You've got everything going for you."

"I haven't got time," I say, a vague guilt clawing my intestines.

The show host asks the guest who s/he picked. Number two. The audience groans. Obviously the wrong choice. The TV camera zeros in on Video Face Number Two, who turns into a live act. "How're you doing back there?" the Host always asks, never waiting for a reply. "Make yourself comfortable." Sure. Get comfortable. How can they, when they know what's coming?

—So, the Show Host says, tell me about your date.

—I knew it the moment I saw him. A total mistake.

What insight. I really must learn to be an instant judge of character. What a timesaver. In my fragile relationships, time is a stopwatch set to four weeks. Sometimes, I self-destruct before the buzzer.

The phone rings again. This time I pick it up. "Shane, you've got to quit calling. What if Tara were here?"

"Tara's at work. And besides, I don't care if she hears it. I'm going to tell her anyway."

"Don't you dare."

"Let me in or I'll call her right now."

I sigh. "All right. All right. But real short. I'm busy." I press the buzzer.

He walks in, casual, goes to stand in front of the TV. "What are you watching?"

"What do you want?" I say.

"I want you."

"You've got Tara."

"I want you," he repeats.

"We've been through all this," I say. "I thought you understood."

"Don't you have *any* feelings?" He stares hard at me.

"Are you done?" My voice is cold.

"Sure, I'm done." He turns and leaves quietly.

I've missed the first half of the show, the first half of my life. I'm watching now. Male guest, female videos; female guest, male videos. No chance of an identity crisis here.

The guest is a middle-aged woman. Short black hair. Thin frame fitted into a strapless spandex dress. A bodysuit. Each time the woman moves her arms, her shoulder bones poke against the skin. Straining to rip through. I imagine I'm watching a skeleton through the x-ray glasses I sent away for, from the back of a Superman comic book.

I pull the skin on my arm. My body suit is opaque. All the better to hide the multicoloured manipulations with, my dear.

—Let's hear what our contestant has to say.

—I want a girl who's 5′ 7″ and doesn't talk much.

An old song surfaces: "My girl Lollipop/ She makes my heart go giddyup…" For Christ's sakes, at least call them women, I shout.

The audience votes. There is laughter and chatter. Pass on all of them, I say. A real timesaver.

Tara and I are lying in bed. It should be dark, as night is, but instead, the room is a glow of muted coral and writhing shadows. Between the streetlamp and our bedroom window is an apple tree, knobby and bent from lack of pruning. The light glares through the thin peach curtains and leaves sharp, defined shadows on the walls, ceiling and dressers. Sometimes, when I can't sleep, I watch these black shapes, often delicate limbs climbing lazy on the ceiling, or paper doilies swaying on the walls—a surreal, live Chinese painting.

"Tara?" I whisper now.

She does not move. I stare at the wall of her back against my face.

I get up and go into the bathroom. Turn on the taps, lie in the bathtub and watch the lurid details of my life smothered in the steam. I am tonight's guest.

—Tell us about your date.

—We met and parted, met and parted, met and… It's safer, you know.

—Couldn't ask for more.

—I could.

Tara stands at the door. "You and Shane," she says.

"It's not true," I lie. "What did he say?"

"He didn't say much. He didn't have to. It's perfectly obvious."

46

"Tara, you've got to believe me. It didn't mean anything."

"That's the most despicable thing I've ever heard you say. For love, I could understand. But to play with my life on one of your meaningless whims—"

"It wasn't just me, you know," I say, defensive.

"You could have stopped it. You shouldn't have allowed it to happen. I'm your sister. Is nothing sacred?"

"Tara, I'm sorry."

"It's too late," she says, and walks out of the bathroom.

I pull my heel out of the drain, and listen to the rhythmic gurgle of water escaping; watch bubbles slowly dissolve into a thin, transparent stream.

I pack one suitcase and my bass guitar into the trunk of my car. Tara does not reply when I say goodbye. I go to a phone booth, call my agent and talk to his wife; arrange to stay with them until we leave on Sunday. She tells me they're going to The Commodore to see the last set of a new band, and asks me to meet them there. I get back in the car and drive for half an hour, out to the university, around the Endowment Lands, Point Grey; park at Jericho beach. Timewasters. Finally, I head downtown.

I find my agent standing at the bar. "Hey, babe," he says. "Howya doin?" and continues without waiting for a reply. "Had a good rest?"

"Sure," I say, slipping into character.

"Here. Have one of these. It'll pick you up."

I swallow it without looking at it.

"All set for the road?" he says.

"Sure," I say. "I'm all set."

Signs

6 AM Sunday morning. They pick me up in a beat-up Econoline van, having driven all night after their gig, these two young women: one barely twenty, one nearly 30. I huddle on a makeshift seat between them. We form a perfect chord, five years apart. Nina, the eldest, is dark and stocky, but wears sensuality in her eyes: that unmistakable "come hither" look, even when she's discussing the weather. Sue is blond, thin and nods often.

"Ever driven a van?" Nina asks from the passenger seat.

"I own one," I say.

"Good. Sue, pull over," she orders, then turns to me as the van slows to a stop. "Sue doesn't have a driver's licence, and mine was suspended two weeks ago. Impaired. You'll be doing the driving from now on."

"Fine," I say. We exchange seats without getting out.

I turn the key, then test the brakes, the clutch, the lights, the signals, the high and low beams, the emergency flashers and the gears.

"It only shifts into second when the acceleration is right. There's a leak in the brake cylinder, but if you pump them, no problem. Just remember to top up the fluid every two or three fill-ups," Nina says, matter-of-fact.

On the way to the gig, we hold a rehearsal. Sue hands Nina an acoustic guitar and a list of songs. Nina reads titles. If I know the song, we go to the next one. If I don't, she plays a few bars on her guitar, stating key signatures and breaks. She puts asterisks beside these so we can rehearse them at the hotel tonight.

I dictate the titles of songs I sing, and she makes a list of these (with asterisks beside the ones she doesn't know). Sue says nothing. She's the drummer. Pair of sticks in hand, she beats out rhythms, using her thigh as snare drum and the back of my seat as ride cymbal. She adds the bass drum rhythms vocally, in monotone grunts—DO DO-DO, DO DO-DO—deep in the throat. A sound that reminds me of a record of Inuit women breathing into each other's mouths. I memorize her rhythms; my bass will give them pitch.

"So, what's happened to your band?" Nina asks when we've gone through the list and practised all the harmonies.

I shrug. "Same old thing. You know. One of the guys in the band. Got a bit too heavy for my liking. What happened to your bass player?"

Nina and Sue exchange amused glances. Then Nina says, "She was too young. Never been on the road. Couldn't hack it, I guess."

By the time we arrive, one thing is clear: Nina is the leader. At the hotel, I'm surprised I have my own room while they share one. If there's a shortage, the band leader always gets special privileges. I'm accustomed to getting my own room, having worked only in male bands.

Weeks pass like schedules stringing time together. When we play at night, the rooms are packed. An all-girl band draws more than drinkers and music lovers. The peripherals:

—critics who grudgingly admit, "You're pretty good," then can't help adding, "for a female band."

—agents armed with slick talk and slippery promises. "A management contract. Only 20% plus expenses."

—men with macho complexes, "How do you three little things manage to move such heavy equipment?"

—reporters, "Whatever made you decide to play bass guitar? Did you have an older brother?" and

—oglers—three women on a stage make good erotic fantasies. I make myself smile, switch to automatic and let my fingers do the playing. The clubowners sell drinks; the audience comes back night after night.

Being a performer, I've discovered, renders you invisible. Men speak about you in the third person. Unlike literature, this does not create identification. Overheard conversation:

"I'd like to take that one home."

I am standing no more than three feet away from their table.

"Too stuck-up. Hasn't talked to anyone all week."

"I wonder what's her problem?"

Shellshocked, buddy, that's my problem. Or men like you. What would you do if you could take me home? A stray dog chasing cars, never expecting to catch them. I'll keep this stance, you keep your distance.

"You got something against men?" Nina says.

"Not particularly."

"Clubowner's been bitching. You've got to work the room."

"Listen," I say, "he pays me to play music and that's what I do."

"They want to talk to you. Christ, you've been in this business long enough. It's good PR."

"Yeah. Well. Tell him to hire a PR person."

This is what happens when I do PR on the breaks. Twenty Questions:

What's your name?

Where are you from?
Are you married?
How long have you been playing?
Is one of the band members your boyfriend?
You got a place we can go do some coke?
What're you doing later?
Etc. etc. etc.

I nod. And nod. And nod.

Eighth week. Accommodations: a bandhouse across the lane from the club. Not too secure. The backdoor has been kicked open so often, only screw holes remain where the various locks were installed along the edge of the door. A two-by-four now slides into metal brackets mounted onto the beams of the doorframe.

Inside, I wait for Nina to choose the best room for herself. She inspects each, only glances at the one with the single bed, then tests the mattresses of the double-beds in the other two rooms. She chooses the room with the largest closet. I've already begun to move my things into the single-bed room, when Nina says, "Why don't you take the one with the double bed?"

"What about Sue?" I ask.

"She's bedding with me."

"Oh."

"You didn't know?" Nina says, then laughs deep in her throat.

"How *would* I know?" There must have been signs.

"Christ," Nina says.

In the middle of the night, I wake up suddenly to no certain sound. Nina is standing in my bedroom doorway, in a thin, synthetic nightgown rendered invisible by the hallway light behind her. I see the dark outline of her body, the thick thighs.

"Is something wrong?" I ask.

She laughs the deep growl of a cat, stares a moment longer, then turns and shuts the door behind her.

In the morning, I look for signs. Nina ignores me at the table, coffee in one hand, *People Magazine* in the other. Sue stands behind her, massaging her neck, then bends and kisses her earlobe.

"Christ," I say.

The next two nights I awake to an apparition of Nina in the doorway. Both times I say nothing, feign sleep. On the third night, I'm too nervous to fall asleep. I hear them in the next room—giggling, moaning, shouting—and pull the blankets over my head, uncomfortable with these intimate sounds of lovers. Then silence. I toss in a restless sleep; fall into a sinister dream:

It is night, and I'm riding on top of an old-fashioned waggon. The road is muddy and rutted, and jolts me off-centre. I am heading somewhere, on a matter of great importance: I must reach the exact middle of a city, and stand on the spot where east-west and north-south intersect. There is no urban development. Fields sprawl on either side of the highway, dotted with scattered barns and farmhouses. Black, black night. There are bonfires everywhere, and the black shapes of men hurling logs. Furtive movements. I am afraid. I huddle on the waggon, trying to make myself invisible. The waggon jolts from side-to-side. I hold on, to offset

the weight of a body sinking on the bed. I begin to sit up, confused. The waggon jars on a rutted trail. Dark night. A sliver of light from the hall slices the quilt. Nina leans over me, so close I can smell the whisky on her breath. In one quick movement, she grabs the top of the quilt and pulls it off me. Instant reaction: I slap her, hard, on the face. She hesitates, then slowly begins to laugh. I pull the blankets up to my chin.

"Get out of here," I say.

Another sound. Sue is a thin silhouette crying in the doorway. Nina gets up, still laughing, and leaves, pushing Sue in front of her.

I shut the door behind them and prop a chair under the door handle, like they do in the movies. I hear shouts, doors slamming, knocks, more shouts, sobs, then moans, groans. I cover my ears.

In the morning, I stay in my room until Nina shouts, "Rehearsal in five."

I come out dressed, wary.

"New song," she says. "Wrote it last night. It's called, 'Don't You Want Me Baby?' "

"Human League beat you to it a few years back," I say.

She laughs. "About last night. I'm sorry. I was a bit drunk."

"A bit," I say.

Nina drinks a fifth of whisky every night between the first and last song. Four hours. For Nina, being a bit drunk is like being a bit pregnant.

"I didn't mean any harm," she says.

The phone rings. A boy, Sue's age. Smitten with her. Nina and Sue don't advertise their sexual persuasion. Not good for PR. Sue hangs up, excited.

"He's got a litter of puppies, and he's going to let me choose one," she says. "Irish setters. Six weeks."

"Oh sure," Nina says. "Just what we need on the road."

"It's only two more weeks. I'll look after it."

"The guy just wants to get into your pants," Nina says.

"You're jealous." Sue laughs.

"Huh. What can he give you?"

Sue dances in front of Nina, taunts her. "About this much," she says, holding her hands six iches apart.

Nina slaps at Sue's hands, a little harder than necessary. Sue slaps back, and suddenly they're wrestling on the ground, angry, excited, I'm not sure what. A violent foreplay.

Bizarre, the spectacle unfolds. Sensational as a *National Enquirer* headline. Their physicality resists the female stereotype, and renders friendly, benevolent, spiritual sisterhood as a dyslexic, fiendly, violent, ritual sinisterhood.

"You got something against women?" Nina asks.

I am barricaded in my room. "Go away."

"Think about it. Nobody knows you better than another woman."

"Some of my best friends are women," I say, sarcastic.

"Just let me in there and I'll show you what you're missing."

"All I'm missing right now is sleep. Go away."

"You won't know until you've tried it."

I open the door. "Listen," I say, "I don't want to try it. I'm not interested. So quit it. I respect your privacy. You respect mine."

"Can I come in?" she says, and laughs.

Disconcerting, this lack of control. The etiquette of courting is well understood by men and women. Observed by both in most cases. No man has ever been so persistent with me, at least not overtly. Especially after blunt refusals. Nina keeps me off balance. Physically threatened. Of what?

"Tomorrow night after the gig, I'm going to his house to get my puppy," Sue says.

"Over my dead body," Nina answers.

"Start digging."

Morning. Nina is in a foul mood. I'm in my room practising, but I can hear her, though I'm wearing headphones. She's in the kitchen slamming cupboard doors, dropping pot lids, throwing cutlery into the stainless-steel sink. Washing dishes, I assume. And making sure we know about it. Nina's housechores are always done by Sue, while Nina smokes cigarettes and delivers a running commentary on Sue's progress. An interesting division: the two of them observing male and female stereotypical roles. This morning, however, Sue is in the living-room, making preparations for her puppy. She was up early, went to Safeway down the block, and returned with six cans of puppy food, a double dog-dish and two large empty boxes. One she has lined with papers for a litter box, and the other with towels (above Nina's objections) for a bed. Through the open door of my room, I watch her humming and fussing, like a mother awaiting her firstborn.

Around midday I come out of my room to make soup and find Nina at the kitchen table, bottle of whisky in front of her half empty. She is writing lyrics in her songbook, and doesn't look up when I come in.

Sue is lying on the couch in the living-room reading a book entitled, *How to Care For Your New Puppy.* Now and then, she reads sections out loud, asks us to comment.

"It says here that I should have a clock wrapped up in a towel next to the puppy," she calls out, "so it thinks it can hear its mother's heartbeat. Do you think I should get a clock?"

"Oh, for Christ's sakes," Nina says, and slams her glass against the tabletop, spilling some of the whisky.

"What's with you, anyway?" Sue says. She comes into the kitchen and stares at the half-empty bottle. "Starting a bit early, aren't you?"

"Early for what?" Nina says.

Sue picks up the bottle, caps it and takes it with her to the living-room.

"Give it back," Nina shouts.

"Go sleep it off."

Nina follows her into the living-room, mouth yakking: Who do you think you are telling me what to do it's my bottle I paid for it what do you care anyway think you're smart cause some little weasel's giving you a puppy yak yak yak etc. etc. etc., culminating in what sounds like a wrestling match, squeals, then giggling.

"I'm sick of it," I shout from the kitchen.

They laugh. And laugh. And laugh.

A perverse sardonic soundtrack to a depraved malignant movie I'm forced to watch. Faces contorted. Gestures grotesque. Caricatures of caricatures. A Fellini movie paling by comparison.

Nina is late for the gig. Bloodshot eyes, matted hair, she kicks the empty bottle out into the hall where it rocks in diminishing arcs against the baseboard.

The night passes slowly. Nina is on her second bottle. Each set is a tortuous disarrangement of discords. The dancefloor is full; audience oblivious to the obscene sound that passes for music tonight. Nina leans against her amp, staring at her fretboard as if it were a foreign object whose function escapes her. Now and then, her fingers drop onto the strings, producing a cacophony of overtones. I reach for her amp and turn off the volume. She doesn't even notice. Sue and I play the last three songs of the night as a bass and drum duo.

Sue's friend waits for her at the side of the stage. She leaves with him, without looking at Nina. I do the cowardly thing—accept an invitation to go for pizza with a young man whose name I can't remember although he's been talking at me for the past three breaks.

Conversation is a Theme & Variations on Twenty Questions. I make myself smile, switch to automatic and let my lips do the rest.

When I've eaten as much as I can for as long as I can, there's nothing left to do but go home. At the door, the young man leans toward me, but I move back. He waits for me to open the door, then says goodnight.

It is 3.43 AM and Sue has not returned yet. I keep looking at the clock, and at Nina who has been stalking me for the past half-hour, even since I came home. We're both sitting at the kitchen table and I'm feigning a passionate interest in the song she wrote this morning. I encourage her to read me the lyrics, explain in detail the reference behind every line, get her guitar and play it for me. I offer suggestions for breaks, for solos, for bass parts; propose revisions on the chorus, arrange harmonies. And all the time I'm looking at the clock behind her and wondering where the hell Sue is. I'm exhausted and I can't keep this up much longer. Fortunately, Nina is so drunk, she can't concentrate and her words are slurred. I make her repeat everything.

Now and then, she has moments of lucidity; her eyes brighten and she slides her hand under the table onto my thighs. I slap at it, and she laughs, muttering, "Soon."

In these moments, I feel powerless, afraid. I'm no match for her, drunk as she is. I make myself smile, switch to automatic, and let my words do the talking. Yak yak yak. Conducting an inner monologue: there's nothing to be afraid of, she's a woman, what can she do, so she might touch you, big deal, she's only a woman, what can she do, there's nothing to be afraid of.

A key turns in the lock. I sigh and get up. Nina lunges at me with such force, she knocks me to the ground, landing on top of me. I beat my fists against her.

Sue stands in the doorway. "You couldn't wait, could you?" she says, and begins to cry.

"For Christ's sakes, get her off me," I shout, arms flailing.

But Sue translates these signs into her language of love. "I hate you both," she screams. "I hate you both."

I kick and punch and thrash.

Nina laughs. And laughs. And laughs.

Off the Road

We arrive at first light. Red Deer, Alberta. The hotel is a beaten building, fifties style, whose colour might have once been a rich brick. Now, the paint has curled off in strips and weathered the wood, creating striped achromatism. The lower part of the building is streaked with mud, gravel and small stones lodged into the wood—a result of many winter sandings of roads. There are two entrances to the bar above which, although no longer functional, signs proclaim, *Men Only* and *Ladies and Escorts*.

What did the women do? I ask no-one in particular.

Come on. It's too early for that crap, Derek says.

We press the buzzer at the side of the door and stand, shivering, in the frost of dawn: a dishevelled, weary troupe, the night drive bruised into our faces.

Six rings and still no reply. Derek leans on the buzzer while the rest of us stamp our feet for warmth. Our breaths are puffs of white; evidence that we are alive. A live. A live what?

I stare into the lobby through the window, which fogs so quickly, I have to keep wiping it with the arm of my coat.

He's coming, I say. Lay off the buzzer.

The desk clerk unlocks the door, opens it a crack, peers at us, then at the van.

We're the band, Derek says.

Yeah. The clerk shrugs. He gives the door a push, and Derek grabs it. We follow him inside. The clerk is clearly not amused by our intrusion.

Your rooms aren't ready, he says. You can't unload now. Too much noise. *Normal* people are *sleeping*, you know.

We sign in and get our keys. There are no coffee shops open. We sit in the dim light of the lobby, and smoke cigarettes. Tonight, we will be stars.

Mid-week. Morning.

I've got to get off the road, I say aloud, to myself.

Derek is sleeping beside me. Ten ounces of scotch buys morning dreams despite the disruptive familiar noises: the jukebox in the bar below emits muffled bass rhythms that begin at noon, precisely, to accompany the strippers; outside the window, trucks idle, while unloading produce, hauling garbage away, picking up laundry, delivering it; the clipped voices of employees—commands, instructions, gossip, arguments—urgent and hurried in the process of business. The bandrooms always face the alleys, the back, directly above the service entrance of any hotel. If you open the window, a mixture of smells assaults you: cooking grease, air-conditioning fluid, laundry soaps, furnace oil, exhaust fumes, rotting garbage, whatever.

I'm lying in bed, staring up. The ceiling is a turbulent ocean whose speckles are treacherous whitecaps, whirlpools I must traverse. I envision a route, beginning at one corner; the superhuman

58

strength I'd need to swim against the monolithic thrust of the sea—currents, tides, constant and relentless.

Wake up. I nudge Derek. You're sleeping your life away.

He pulls the pillow over his head.

Saturday night. Crisis night. During the second set, a waitress hands me a note on which is written our agent's name, phone number and CALL IMMEDIATELY. Derek reads it over my shoulder, then shrugs. I hold up the note for Jason and Paul to see. Drummer and keyboard player. We all know what it means. An agent only calls on a Monday (after the first set) if the clubowner wants to fire the band, or on a Saturday night to tell you next week's gig has fallen through. There is always an alternate gig, at lower money, further distance. Sink or swim. Stuck in the middle of nowhere. Rent to pay back home. Massive operating expenses on the road—PA rentals, truck and trailer rentals, light and sound man on contract, etc. etc. He's got you and he knows it.

We hold a band meeting after I've phoned him. It's the only time we talk now. The band members, I mean. And when we rehearse and need to communicate each other's shortcomings. We're polarized: Derek and I on one side; Jason and Paul on the other. Funny thing, can't pinpoint why. Except, maybe, Derek and I share a room. We haven't come such a long way, baby. The males are still spraying territory.

It's in Fort St. John, I say.

That's through Pine Pass, Jason adds, as if we didn't know.

We haven't even got snow tires, Paul says.

We'll jacknife the fucking trailer. Jason forms a V with his hands.

So what are we going to do for a week? Derek asks.

He's got a point. Here we are, into December. We've been on the road since the middle of October. Who's got money for a week layover?

Well, I don't like it one bit, Jason says. I think we should put our foot down.

What do you suggest? I ask.

Tell the sleaze to shove his gig. We'll book our own.

It's Saturday night, I point out. How're we going to get a gig next week?

Canadian Tire's open on Sundays, Derek says. We can buy chains. Cheaper than snow tires.

We continue this pointless discussion. Half-hearted. Replaying a scene. Each of us has his part memorized. In the end, we all know we'll agree to do the gig.

You want a drink? Derek asks, putting an end to it.

Sure. Big enough to drown in.

Lay off, Jason says. You better do uppers. We got a long drive.

When I call the agent back, he's not the least surprised. He probably contracted us into that gig weeks ago. It's an old agency manoeuvre to ensure the booking of undesirable rooms. Promise cake. Suppress information. Then throw out a few crumbs and watch the scramble. Yet each time, we insist on playing out this little charade—this democratic process of decision—when clearly, there are no options.

Third set. Complete boredom. We haven't switched songs around all week. I've memorized the succession of tunes—a slow crescendo. We spend hours designing set lists in our rooms so that the songs are of varied keys and rhythms. Strung together, they must form the lash of a whip that snaps on the last chord of the last song. Then we take a break.

I'm singing. Derek leans into my ear.

Looking damn good, he says.

I could do you right here, he says.

What say we go up to the room on the break? he says.

I continue to sing. Don't miss a note. Yakety yak. He's been drinking steadily for the past three hours. He's at the sex stage. A couple of hours more, he'll be hunched over his guitar, unable to even talk about it. Easy to get this way. Drinks materialize at the edge of the stage, in front of each musician, increasing as the night progresses until, at lights out, clusters of glasses (empty and full) are all that remain of the band. Ghost markers. Gravestones.

Have another drink, I say.

I've got to get off the road, I think, staring past the spots into the tension of the room. Rubber bands ready to spring. Three-quarters through the night. Few pairups yet. In all bars, there is a collective orchestration of conduct. At the beginning, during the first set, people sit around tables, lean against walls, scrubbed clean, combed, smelling of aftershave, body lotion and familiar perfumes. A polite, reserved group of guests invited to the promise of excitement. With each passing hour, eddies of desperation begin to swirl in their eyes as they search for the fulfillment that has so far eluded them.

If I stare hard enough into the room, I see gusts of unrest. Small-craft warning. If I close my eyes, I feel the undertow of tension. Swim at your own risk.

Bar sales increase. Voices rise, as does the slam of empty glasses on tabletops. On the dancefloor, an octopus of arms and legs, hands squeezing buttocks, shirts unbuttoned, dresses creased, hair dishevelled. The bar, in collective degeneration.

The band, too, is in a state of entropy. At the beginning of a tour, we are united. Adventurers crossing an ocean for the first time. Each week, we touch the shore of a new city, hotel, bar, stage. A succession of conquests. The crowd roars. We respond. Pushing all the right buttons. Savouring each stroke. And soon, we begin to wonder who is conquering who? We are no more/no less than all the bands that inhabit these spaces, which are reduced to anonymity—projected images of an audience who creates us in a collaborative invention; renders us static, imprinted on stages like paintings of nature displayed in art galleries across the globe.

Walk off the stage into a room. Hear adulation. Watch people's eyes not see you. Idolomaniacs worshipping their own illusions.

Music is fisherman's line through the heart. We flail, gasp for air and embrace it in a desperate attempt to define ourselves.

If I squint against the lights, the room becomes a turbulent ocean; red terry tablecloths are crests of waves. The Red Sea.

Middle of the third song, last set: a ripple begins near the door and widens in concentric circles throughout the bar, gaining momentum, until its strength hurls tables one against the other, and topples chairs.

What's going on? I ask Derek after the first chorus.

He stands on tiptoe, chin up. Delivers a brilliant guitar solo I've heard so often I could play it myself (if I could play guitar).

Can't see. Likely a fight over some broad.

I want my own room next place, I say.

He doesn't miss a note; doing a triplet run against four, hammering strings with his fingering hand.

No big deal, he says. It's just a fight.

Crowd moves in, not out in a fight, I say.

Gets into the act. Throws a few punches. Frustration flowing through the arm. Unwitting targets. It's the release that counts. The contact.

I still can't see what's happening. A thick wall of backs is undulating toward us. Ocean waves parting. The bouncers are coastguards shouting directions, monitoring safe passage.

As the crowd nears us, I begin to hear an erratic chorus of voices. Shrieks. Discordant harmonies above the melodic strains of the guitar solo.

We better slow it down, Derek says.

I nod, then glance through the set list to find a ballad in the same key. Smooth transition. We skip the last verse and chorus of the song we're playing, and go directly to the tag after the guitar solo. Jason counts in the ballad while we sustain the last chord. It's in the musician's bible. If trouble starts, the band keeps playing. Slows it down; changes the mood—audience wired into our rhythms.

Fuck, Derek says when we both can see the cause of the commotion.

He is a small wiry man. Taut body. A Roman candle ready to explode into a shower of limbs. He is waving something black in his right hand, and people part to let him through.

A madman with a gun, I say. Let's get the hell out of here.

Keep still, Derek shouts. Keep playing.

And there we are, the four of us, rooted on stage, holding our instruments in front of us like shields.

I've got to get off the road, off the road, off the road, I think, repeating the words in my head like a mantra in time to the rhythm my fingers create. A hypnotic displacement of a heartbeat. What song? I hear my voice through a distant tunnel—someone else mouthing a tune. Long forgotten.

Suddenly, a wave parts at the front of the stage, and the man emerges, a triumphant Moses.

In his hand, he grips a live rat by the tail.

And all is slow motion: his steps toward me, the scramble from nearby tables, the mounting huddle of people at the sides of the room. Some of the women stand on chairs, out of fear, or perhaps to see the action better.

Directly in front of me, the man. Ravaged face. Eyes soiled black. Could be 30 or 50. Tense, bony, swathed in blue jeans and black tank top. A body devouring itself.

For once, the crowd is silent and we are giving a command performance—all eyes have riveted to the stage. Hysteria begins as a cool numbing in my stomach. My fingers are still moving over the bass strings, as if they no longer belong to me. Slowly, I inch my way backwards, toward the drum riser, without breaking the stare between me and the man who stands, challenging, in front of centre stage, rat held out.

One of the bouncers, in a heroic attempt, rushes him from my left. The man turns quickly. Arcs the rat in a semi-circle. I can almost hear bullets splay into the nearby bodies. The bouncer retreats, and the man turns to me again. The rat's high-pitched sounds scurry up my spine. My hands are damp, but clinging to the bass strings. The man laughs. A mocking, ugly reverberation. He swings the rat toward me, like a priest wielding an aspersorium. I recoil.

Take it easy, Derek says. It's only a rat.

And I wonder to whom he is referring, and how these rooms are breeding grounds. The man is a hypnotist. I count his pendulum sways. Four, five, six. Hypnotized by the tiny black head that darts side to side. Suddenly the rat jerks up and sinks its teeth into the man's wrist. The man howls and shakes his arm until the rat falls onto the stage. Confusion is a relief. Within the crowd's collective surge and intake of breath, our music falters to a halt—clusters of ringing overtones. None of us thinks to dampen the strings.

I jump onto the drum riser. Derek stamps his feet. The rat, after a few confused starts, scurries off stage left, then glides onto the floor. The crowd hedges in for a better look, keeping careful, if not polite distance.

I am still staring at the man who continues to howl, but it is no longer from surprise or pain. He is emitting a primal sound—guttural, tortured, inhuman. His eyes are glazed and bulging. Slowly, he stretches his right arm toward me, and I can see a trickle of blood on his inner wrist. I take a deep breath; try to move, but my feet are weights holding me down. There is an echo at the back of my throat. A frightening wave of black threatening.

KEEP PLAYING! The Manager is standing at one end of the stage.

I am holding my breath. Jason counts in the next song on the list, and my fingers respond; curl around the neck of my bass guitar like a life preserver. I am actually singing, standing behind myself, at the edge of a reef.

The bouncers attack; wrestle the man to the ground, amid the sound of scuffles, pounds and shrieks.

The music spills in my open spaces and seals me.

I look down at the floor. One small crumpled man, shoulders shuddering. There is no need for the three bouncers who still hold him in embarrassed silence. The crowd turns away. Straightens chairs. Pushes tables to re-establish social space. Someone shouts for a waitress. A couple move onto the dancefloor.

Imagine the stage, a treadmill set on white sand at low tide. And there we are, keeping time, instruments slung to our bodies. And slowly, as the weeks pass, the tide rises and we move slightly faster, trying to ignore the waves that lick at our feet. And soon our shins are covered. Our movement sluggish. A constant struggle against the weight. And we try to walk faster, feeling the water slowly inch up our thighs—a ring of ice numbing. We are still singing, though the ocean's roar is winning. The weight against the chest is unbearable. We advance, inch by inch, spiralling.

I've got to get off the road, I say.

64

Infinites

So, ask me. What makes a woman pack a bag in the middle of an afternoon and take a taxi to the airport? A man who says ever, never and forever. Trying to turn the infinite into the finite. And succeeding. I'm leaving, aren't I? Infinite and definite. Interesting how "in" is forever and "de" is specific. Although not when it comes to "IN love" or "DElusion." But that's a different story. This one is finite. Sonny. Even the name is ridiculous. As if his mother had no imagination. An encapsulated version:

We were travelling together for some time (musicians, rock

bands—too tedious to go into). He fell into my bed one night in the middle of a song. No point pretending love was any part of it (unless you count his girlfriend in Alberta who sat in their rented apartment waiting for his return). Me too. Waiting, that is, for his return to her. Three weeks is one week too long for consecutive lust. Those ever/never/forevers start materializing between the sheets. INdelible stains. Whispered sometimes, even though the eyes are closed. Of course, despite my protests, or should I say my unveiled cautioning (DON'T tell her, DON'T count on me, DON'T, DON'T), he did and she left.

What do you tell a man who has rashly thrown his passport into the fire and is now watching it burn? What do you tell him when he has nowhere else to go? Dispossessed. You tell him, you can come home with me but *only* if you apply for a new one and *only* until it comes. We drove twelve hours in a van filled with all his possessions.

A temporary stay is one thing. The only way to INsure its temporal state is to forbid comfort. This means rigid enforcement of certain ground rules: no key, no male clothes in my closet, no answering the phone, no giving this as his address (however temporary), no toothbrush in my glass (keep it in your travel-kit) and not even a whisper of a sock falling on the rug.

Rules, by DEfinition, must be tested. How else to establish the bend? Once INvaded, a private space is difficult to DEfend. Imagine for a moment poor Sonny, his 25 years packed into boxes in his van parked outside my apartment. Pathetic, really, that he should hear and not listen.

And now, I'm getting to the airport part. You'll miss your plane. Is it dark already? I'm here because of what happened last night. Two months is time enough for goodbye (why call it good, when it's a dismissal?). Still Sonny's van keeps a space dry in front of the building. Like cows just before a rain. So I told him, get out of my bed. Not too subtle, I know. There are times when words should bludgeon. He said all the buts, I thoughts, didn't wes, couldn't yous, and finally began to pack the few things I allowed him to keep INside: travel-kit, guitar, jacket, one pair of jeans (in the hall closet), address-book, boots, gloves and the bananas he bought in the morning. He fit it all into two 7-Eleven Bags (potato chips-and-cigarette size). No suitcases in here. A little too permanent for my liking. He took a long time doing this. I committed the penultimate sin and went to bed. Closely followed by the ultimate sin—fell asleep. Like arriving home after being trapped in rush-hour traffic for two hours. There's only relief.

The airport part. Yes. I'm getting to it. Well. I was awakened at 3 AM by Sonny's hand on my arm. (Can you tell I haven't slept?) I'm going, he said, I thought I should say goodbye. As if his leaving were an impulsive INvention of his own. Goodbye, I said, pulling the blankets up to my neck. I know the trappings of darkness, in the limbo between sleep and awake. Similar to three drinks of scotch and no food. The body says things the mind can't understand. So I closed my eyes. The better to see you with, my dear.

I don't know where I'll go, he said. I'll call you when I get there.

I pulled the blankets over my head. Couldn't last long though. No air. Makes a dramatic vision, don't you think? WOMAN ASPHYXIATED IN HER OWN BED BY QUILT.

See you around, I said, like a record. Stress makes me say the weirdest things. DEfense mechanism.

You lie, he said, like sidewalk. True, though.

I'll cut it short. This is supposed to be the encapsulated version. (No real dialogue allowed.) All night, he sits on my bed in his jacket, gloves and boots, and says goodbye. Trying to turn the finite into the INfinite. Damn near succeeding. WOMAN ASPHYXIATED IN HER OWN BED BY GUILT.

So, what could I do when in the morning I found him sleeping on the floor beside the bed? Like a scatter-rug. Almost stepped on him. Did, metaphorically speaking. I shut the bedroom door, made coffee and read the paper. Mundane solutions to mundane situations.

It was past noon when he awakened. I walked around him, packed my bag and here I am. So. What kind of solution is this? You might well ask. You might well come home with me. But just for tonight. It might be a solution.

67

Kaleidoscope

How could someone, Gary says, just stand by and let that happen?

It's realistic, I say. Sometimes things are beyond a person's control.

Well, I can't believe any human could be that inhuman.

We've just been to see *The Accused.* A film about rape and the bystanders who watched without intervening.

All the way home we argue. Gary armed with his black and white convictions; I with the grey shadings of human nature. Idealism versus naturalism. We're as different as that. We spend a lot of our time arguing.

What are you looking at? Gary asks later, at home, bending over me.
My different personas.

I'm sitting on the floor, three albums in one pile, the one labelled PROMO SHOTS open in front of me. Black Letraset splashes across the photos. White teeth glisten. Perfect symmetry. LIVE FROM BACEDAS! LIVE FROM THE CAVE! LIVE FROM whatever. Stylish illusions abreast with the times. Created with lenses, lights, gels and umbrella reflectors, on dull afternoons, in empty clubs, where a photographer's patience is directly proportional to the $100 an hour we pay him to turn us into an item. There are photos of me:
  in long sequined gowns (a-la-Cher);
  in black satin hipsters and five-inch heels (a-la-Tina Turner);
  in gold padded shoulders and harem pants (a-la-Patti LaBelle);
  in leather and chains (a-la-psuedo punk).
Like listening to memories. Fragile reproductions that sometimes reverberate. I slam the echoes shut.

There are photos of me, too, being myself. In the other albums. Captured in shutters. Shut her. Like an eye winking after a bawdy joke. Journeys across Canada and back so often, the prints are grouped by names of the provinces. Smiles fixed timeless; borders nudging in the spread of a decade.
LIVE FROM NEWFOUNDLAND. The view from the ferry: jagged rock cliffs pointing arthritic fingers into the sea. Miniature houses perched at odd angles. Fishing boats slammed by the tides into the nailed half-moon tires on the dock.
The Oriana. A beast of burden, female as all ships are. Carrying a crew of 400, I think. We went to see her when she docked. The largest passenger ship in the world and they wouldn't let us board. As if five more would sink it. That was the summer I lost twenty pounds. Cornerbrook, Newfoundland. 1982. In the photo, the Atlantic Ocean is a most unlikely shade of blue. Creme de Menthe swirling in a frosted glass on our last night:

Saturday. A dimly lit nightclub. Slow-motion replay behind my eyelids. Tex and I sitting at the bar, elbow-to-elbow. On a break. Two cigarettes till showtime. Tex lit one and passed it to me. Took another out for himself but didn't light it. Constantly in motion, Tex, even when still. Tight, rigid movements laden with anxiety.

"How do I look?" he asked.

As if he had to ask. As if the hour and half grooming in the bathroom wouldn't show. Black hair gelled straight back, no part. Neck long and pale fitted into the white shirt collar, all meticulously framed by a black pin-striped double-breasted suit.

"Like a gangster," I said.

He smiled. "Do you really think so?"

I stifled a sigh. Or a laugh. So easy to please men.

It was the summer after the spring breakup with Tom. I was determined to turn my life into an adventure—a kaleidoscope. Collide and cope with consequences later. Tex and I performed a sexual fantasy all summer. In hotel-rooms, bathrooms, on buses, in the back seat of the van when everyone slept. Sexual collisions without words, without commitment, with out. (Months later, when he came to Vancouver, he proposed marriage. But I'd gained back the weight by then.)

We were appropriately called FLESH, four male musicians and myself, thrown together like spices from a rack, carefully chosen by an agent to blend into a saleable commodity for mass consumption. Rock bands are seldom a uniting of soulmates, but rather suppliers of illusion, and demand dictates their form. So much for art.

We'd met in Calgary five weeks before: Zinto, Tex, Jerry and Marc, all from Western Canada. Each had left a band to form this one. The agent had paid airfares and rehearsal time—two weeks—then sent us to Eastern Canada. We were working our way back in a ten-week stint. Sink or swim. I held back the agent's commission, in case we hit dry land.

When I tell Gary some of these things, he stares at me with a strange look. As if he doesn't believe what he's hearing. He is not a musician and can't possibly appreciate survival tactics.

For instance, being a woman, a musician and a guitar player, I know all about survival. In the music biz, men are musicians and

70

women are singers. The male musicians outnumber the women ten to one. In order to work, I had to adopt a new thesaurus for survival. Synonyms. Euphemisms. For example, equal means better; acceptance means mute observation. The former, no problem—hundreds of hours of practise—I now receive more work offers than I can accept. Fitting into an all-male band, with its clearly defined unspoken rules, requires silent complicity. If someone were to ask me to describe the lifestyle of rock musicians, I'd probably pause (thinking of vulnerability), then I'd deliver every cliché uttered on the subject. I fit into this lifestyle, a paradox, like the male musicians—no better, no worse. All wrapped parcels of insecurities held together by ribbon, a specious fuse.

Gary and I have been living together for two years. He works in a bookstore and spends his free time campaigning for causes. Seal hunt. Women's rights. Acid rain. Rape victims. Native land claims. Aids. Toxic waste. Nuclear disarmament. Our apartment is a maze of cubbyholes constructed by stacks of leaflets on every social injustice perpetrated by man. We are a most unlikely couple. Gary is solid: a nine-to-five job and perfect ideals. He stands on the left of everything, on principle. I sway with the fluctuations of emotions: romantic, sordid, realistic, whatever the circumstance. Indiscriminate. Gary calls my renditions "operatic melodramas."

That summer with Tex. That night at the bar. The whole trip, Tex and Zinto were bringing home groupies. An intricate game of upmanship. Tex and I fit each other into the spaces. No-one knew. The sordid nature of it made it exciting.

Gary told me that he's never had a one-night stand. It doesn't fit into his conscious image of himself. I censor my past appropriately. Innocent, naïve, self-righteous bastard. If you want to see humanity at its worst, become a musician. Make the rounds. Play the local bars, the lounges, the B-rooms and the A-rooms, the Rock & Roll cabarets, the Blues clubs, the Swanky Hotels, the concert halls. The only difference is the cover charge and the dress code. There's nothing like performance to draw the hangers-on. A great big giant magnet sucking up the dregs. This is life at the bottom. Which only varies from life at the top by the missing digits on the paycheque.

That Saturday night in Newfoundland, in the five minutes before the second set, Tex and I were wrapped in the folds of the left stage curtain. Twenty seconds to spare before the other band members arrived. This is how it was with us. A look. Instant libido. No props needed.

Gary treats love-making like one of his causes. He's well-read on the subject and insists on decorum. Proper clothes, etcetera, straight out of *Playboy*. I could fill another album with these personas.

That Saturday night in Newfoundland, Tex brought a groupie back to the band house. I don't recall her name, only her white halter-dress, flimsy as moth wings. Nothing unusual about her, about all these women who see themselves as conquerors, as if through physical contact with performers, they can transcend their ordinary lives. "Willing victims," I tell Gary who flinches. Icarus flying to the sun. What they don't comprehend is that this sun is created by artificial power—75,000 watts of it. Enough to burn a lot of wax, but only during performance hours.

How did I manage? Played it cool and calm. Tex was the nervous one when we reached the house, went in through the basement, tripped over his bed, clothing, shoes.
"Hey! Watch where you're going. Jesus! Would you get out of here?" Tex shouted to us.
I knew what came next. Tex's Rules of Conduct:
1. He never kissed on the lips (this, he told me, was reserved for love and affection); and
2. he always slept alone (he didn't want to wake up next to a stranger).
If he'd been a lawyer, he'd have made women sign a contract before they took their clothes off.

Gary and I met on New Year's Eve, outside one of the First Night Venues. We were both freezing in the rain, trying to hear an obscure jazz quartet through the open window of a small restaurant. My

friends were inside, unaware that the last ticket had gone to someone two couples ahead of me. Gary, too, had lost his party. We
decided it was fate, linked arms and went in search of a warm bar.
We didn't make love until May. By then, I was hooked on romanticism.

Tex didn't bother with preliminaries. Didn't ask the girl if she
wanted a drink or a coffee, or anything.
    I changed out of stage clothes, put my guitar away, then went
into the living-room. Turned on the the TV and flicked channels
until I found an old movie *Dr. Jekyll & Mr. Hyde*—Spencer Tracy,
Lana Turner and Ingrid Bergman. I got my pillow, then lay on the
couch to watch the last half. Jerry and Marc were playing chess. An
on-going game, the nights they came home alone.
    Zinto paced the room. Restless. He towered over Marc and
Jerry; watched them for a bit (although we all knew he couldn't play
chess), then went back to the kitchen. I could hear him make a
sandwich—fridge door opened and closed three times; cutlery
drawer sliding in and out; freezer compartment for the bread;
wooden board slammed against the counter. Finally, he returned
with a stacked sandwich on a plate, and sat across from me. "You
know what I'd really like to do?" he said between bites. "I'd really
like to go and see the ocean. It's only about fifteen miles away. I
want to see the Atlantic ocean. You guys wanna go?'
    "Sure, Zinto. Only it's too dark to see the ocean." Jerry yawned.
"Let's go tomorrow."
    Zinto finished his sandwich, then went to the window, shed-
ding his clothes on the way, until he was down to his underwear.
"Fuck, it's hot in here." He sat back down and watched part of the
movie with me.

There's no point pretending I was totally unaffected. When I got
home to Vancouver at the end of the summer, my bathroom scales
tipped at 90. I'm 5 feet 5 inches tall. Figure it out. My friends were
convinced I was anorexic; my doctor thought I should be hospital-
ized; I swallowed Valiums, stayed home and ate for a month in
front of the TV. Completely cured. But gun shy. So much for kalei-
doscopes.

I suddenly think that maybe if I told Gary all this, we'd never argue again. If I could only show him that these photos, these personas are glossy, static optical illusions. Sustainers of strangers' fantasies. Mine too.

But this is yet another fantasy. Gary wears his costume of liberalism woven from his various causes. There are photos of him among the homeless, the aged, the alcoholics, the prostitutes, spearheading campaigns to save them from the evils of society. A self-proclaimed Saviour. The Second Coming. But at home he would not tolerate the defilement of his pristine values, his puritan mind and immaculate soul.

If only one could see both oceans at once. That night in Newfoundland, the basement door opened and Tex came up the stairs alone. The girl had shed her moth wings and passed out, virtue intact.

This is the part I don't want to recall. I must have tried to stop them. Zinto, Jerry and Marc. The thumps of their boots on the stairs. Like a migraine returning. When a baboon knows it's cornered, it covers its face and awaits the attack. There were no screams to pierce the conscience.

I lay on the couch and tried to concentrate on the movie. Only Tex and I were left.

"Can't you stop it?" I asked.

"Come on. It's no big deal. She came here to get laid."

"But she's unconscious."

"Small difference."

I remained on the couch and Tex came and sat beside me. He touched my shoulders, then leaned over and kissed me gently on the lips. Startled, I pushed him away, got up and went to the kitchen to make coffee. I took a long time doing this. A tightness began in my belly, though I tried to ignore it. When I returned to the living-room, the movie credits were rolling and Tex said, "I'm going to bed."

I didn't answer, and lay back down on the couch. A second movie began, but I couldn't concentrate. I thought about going to bed and forgetting the whole thing. There was nothing I could have done. I went into Jerry's room and found something to calm me down. He was a virtual pharmacy, Jerry. Whatever you had, he could cure; whatever you lacked, he could supply.

Some time passed. I fell asleep and was awakened by laughter, followed by footsteps. Marc and Jerry came in and resumed their chess game, as if nothing had happened. The second movie ended. Sign-off. "O Canada." In both official languages. Then snow. Jerry got up and turned off the TV. I stared out the window at the pinkish hues on the underlayer of clouds.

Funny how things turn out. When you least expect it, antonyms: strangers become lovers and lovers become strangers.

Gary comes into the room and stares at me staring at the photos.

Are you still looking at those? he asks. There are more important things in the world.

Not to me right now.

What is it then?

A rather sordid memory. Do you want to hear it?

No, he says. Not when you're in one of those moods.

The same, perhaps, as I felt that night when Zinto padded, barefoot, into the room, wrapped in a dressing-gown. "She's awake, boys."

Marc and Jerry grinned. No one looked at me. I might have been invisible. "She thought I was Tex," Zinto said. "She's getting dressed. No problem. She'll never know."

"I think I'll go crash," Marc said.

"No you don't. We're going to see the ocean. It's light now." Zinto walked to the window. "We'll drive her home."

"That's big of you," I said, and they all three turned to me.

"You stay out of this. Not a word."

When she came into the living-room, I picked imaginary lint off my jeans.

"Hello," Zinto said in his casual voice. "We've been up all night. Coffee's hot. You want some?"

She nodded, nervously trying to smooth her hair.

"Listen, that bastard Texas just couldn't wait any more. Went to bed and asked if I'd drive you home. I won't let anyone drive the van, you know. It's my baby. What a bastard! You don't mind, do you?"

"That'll be fine." She stared at me, but I looked away.

"Anyway," Zinto continued, "we're off to see the ocean. Never seen the Atlantic. What a bastard thing to do, that Tex. Got no class. He said to say goodbye."

The girl sipped her coffee, sitting stiffly on the armchair, while Zinto casually dressed.

It was almost dawn. The van's windows were wet with dew. The girl's dress fluttered against the seat. We drove her home, then continued out to the ocean.

On the beach, we stood together. The photograph shows me in the middle, my arms around Zinto and Marc's shoulders, while in the background the sun slashes the water with a crimson blade.

B-Grade Movies

I'm standing in the cool night air. Two things happened to me today. So I figure, why not cause the third, then I can relax. I know this isn't matches and war. Well. Perhaps it is about matches. Or mismatches.

Number one concerns Gary. We have been living together for two years, stuck in an old movie now in syndicated reruns. Brief personal details about Gary for context: he trims his toenails every Thursday night before taking a shower; he can accurately type 87 words a minute without using a Spellcheck; and he views everything as black or white, leaving no room for possibilities.

So what happens is this: I'm lying in bed, thinking *apathy*. Not the concept, just the word. Meaningless. And suddenly, it becomes transparent. A window. Stare through it long enough and you forget it's there. Like riding on a train, watching landscape hurtling in reverse. And there I am, in stationary mode, observing the chaotic race to an uncertain past. Standing still. Going backwards. Back words. Fitted to music, they transport you to distant pasts and brief intimacies.

Which brings me to number two: Lenny. Distant, past, brief and intimate. A guitar player. That's the music part. Window blurs. And there we are in a B-grade black & white movie. Cigarette smoke swirls between our faces. We're saying goodbye. No. That's the problem. We never did really say goodbye. Picture it yourself. It's an old storyline: we're on the road together; he has a wife back home; he wants us both. I fall in love; suffer a while; then leave him. Predictable ending. Only difference, I don't die.

Ever noticed how there are only two kinds of women in these movies? Ones men love and ones men marry? And how heroic the men are in their transgressions? Tortured souls. Creatures of integrity. Choosing between love and responsibility. Of course, the women are punished (implication being it's *their* fault): one sentenced to ruin or death for love; the other sentenced to a loveless marriage. The men get both women, and ride into the sunset— unscathed heroes. Have a Kleenex.

So there I am, in bed, blankets over my head, posturing drama. Choreographed into another B-grade movie. Christ. I've always been much better at freestyle. You know this storyline too: woman must choose between man and career. No juggling in these movies. It's an either/or. Picture blurs. Time passage. A year:

Either you spend some time in town, Gary says, *or* we're through.

Double ambiguity. Either/ors are ultimatums thinly disguised as choices. It only takes an "n" to expose them for what they really are: neither/nors. So I choose one, and we call it a (com)promise. Though what Gary promises, I don't know. Imagine for a moment the scene:

It is morning. The man is leaving for work. The woman stands at the door, wearing a demure dark dress with a white lace collar.

On her feet, spiked sandals—a symbol of her former life. The man strokes her cheek, gives her a condescending smile as if to say, "the naughty girl has been saved in spite of herself." Violins. She waves, dewy-eyed. He drives to work smug in his heroic deed. Unblemished. The audience stirs, perhaps a little saddened that so virtuous a man could love such a woman. There's never any marriage in these movies, although he might propose in the final scene, but only when he discovers that she *either* has an incurable disease *or* has been fatally injured in an accident. She dies in his arms. Final closeup: man's face, stoic. One tear rolls down his cheek. Credits. Have another Kleenex.

Well. I'm very much alive. Still wearing spiked sandals. Still think Laura Ashley dresses make good bedspreads. However, I'll admit, I fell into part of that movie. You see, Gary came along not too long after Lenny and, hey, he sure looked good, comparatively speaking. Organized. He took over my life and managed it like his. I let him. Truth is, I needed a little managing. Too many jagged edges. And there's nothing like a straight man. Ploughs a narrow road. You just put one foot in front of the other. No falling in ditches.

So. Not only did I come off the road, I had to go solo. For a band to work permanently in town is as difficult as falling in love. Band and audience unite in infatuation, each wary of the other. There is always another band, another club. And both, once hot, can only cool. Distance remedies this. Thus, the road. One-nighters. No fear of commitment.

Solo performances. So low, you're licking the ground. We're talking major adjustment here. Lounges. Main difference between nightclub and hotel lounge: a nightclub has a stage. In a band, you stand on the platform, much like inhabiting an island—the audience is a froth that wets the shores only. But in a hotel piano bar, you have no elevation. Only the music lifts you.

Brief lounge scene for context. In Technicolor:

First night. Every Monday is a first night. Every Saturday a last. In this business, one clearly understands the finite property of things. The Manager is waiting for me at the bar and, when I ask him where I should set up, he says, "*Either* against that mirror *or* the one opposite it."

Mirrors reflect sound. I say, "How about next to the curtain? That'll absorb overtones."

"The mirrors are better," he says, "because the audience can see your back too."

Great. "Perhaps I could wear a backless dress and paint a happy face between my shoulder-blades," I say.

"Ha. Ha. Ha," he says.

Playing in a lounge is like performing at an institute for the deaf. Vision and touch are the primary senses. I smile and duck.

Once, while on a break, a man asked why I was alone ("What's a good-looking woman like you doing in this place all by yourself?"), and when I told him ("Playing music for lonely alcoholics"), he either didn't hear or chose to ignore my comment, and said, "Really? I thought it was the jukebox." And when I said, "It was. I was only lip-synching," he believed me. Later, he sat in front of me and watched.

Fade out.

And this, too, is a solo sequence. Set in a dingy hotel-room. And there we are, Lenny and I, scraping bottom. A non-verbal scene. No musical score here. The spaces grow larger than the action. Tension device. We need music in movies for aural clues. How else to understand the visuals—selected incidents, which strung together form characters' lives? Button pushers. Clue #1: orchestration: violin = romance; saxophone = sex; banjo = freedom; oboe = regret; flute = joy; and so on. Clue #2: chord construction: major scale = love; blues scale = sorrow; minor scale = melancholy; suspended chords = tension; diminished and augmented chords = expectation; and so on. Even the terminology is perfect.

In this scene, there are only excruciating silences, punctuated by the slam of glasses on night-tables, gaining in violence as the minutes pass. The man and the woman sit apart. They do not even look at each other. Their only connection is the scotch, which they pour into glasses from the bottle between them.

The scene you won't see is the one that happens later, in the darkness. When their bodies scream and claw to a Stravinski score. One drowning and pulling the other under. Interchangeable and destructive.

Fast-forward. Back to this morning. There I am, lying in bed, languishing like a tragic heroine. Thing is, I'm bored with black & white movies. And the phone rings and it's Lenny and we haven't talked for at least eight months and he wants to see me. So I tell him where I'm playing and he says he'll come to the hotel tonight.

Which he does, near the end of my first set. He sits at the piano across from me. He is wearing black T-shirt, black jeans, black leather jacket. I recognize him in the movie as the adventurer, the magnetic pull to the dark side.

"How are things?" he says.

"Great." I switch to an instrumental. "You still playing?"

He lights a cigarette. "Just got off the road. Got a few gigs in town coming up."

"Same band?" I ask.

"Na. Rob split a couple of weeks after you did, and we had to pick up a drummer in Calgary. Not bad." He drags on his cigarette, then lets the smoke tunnel from his nose. "You thinking of joining a band?" He says it casually, but I know different.

"Haven't thought about it." I finish the instrumental and keep my left hand going while I flip pages in my cheat book for the next tune. My mind has gone blank.

"You still do 'When a Man Loves a Woman?'" he asks.

"On occasion."

"You used to do that great."

I find it alphabetically, and begin the intro. A waitress comes to take his order. I shut my eyes while I sing.

In the movies, adventurers always end up alone. But the nuance is different, according to gender. A lone woman languishes in loneliness; a lone man thrives in freedom. The audience roots for the guy at home. No matter that she's unhappy. Well. Women don't know their minds. She's obviously confused. Give her a good hard look at this loser, and she'll come to her senses.

When I look up at the end of the song, Lenny is staring at me. He's looking like a winner: a tall, lean, mean machine. Oops. Modern movie slipped in. He pats the stool beside him and taps the edge of the scotch glass in front of it.

I take a break; go and sit with him at the other side of the piano.

"The band's doing a few of my originals," he says. "We're hoping to do a demo while we're in town."

"Sounds great," I say, trying to muster enthusiasm. It's an old story. I've heard it, I've told it and I've rarely believed it in either mode.

One of the regulars comes to sit on the stool beside me. Intruding. On purpose. Regulars don't like musicians speaking to strangers. They force themselves between, for inclusion. In the movies, a conflict device. Delay the action. What will the hero and heroine say to each other when they can? Tension mounts.

The regular's name is Dave. He introduces himself to Lenny and shakes his hand, all the while staring at me. Making a statement. Then he orders a round.

Lenny swirls the ice against the sides of his glass. A familiar gesture: he wants to talk to me alone, but can't say so. I've learned to read men's body language. Only way to survive. I think about Gary, who always says exactly what he means. So specific, there's no room for conjecture. I've always chosen men with thin skin, moods visible just below the surface. Gary is opaque. Impenetrable. His calm unsettles in me a powerful need for disruption.

"Would you play 'Memory' for me?" Dave asks.

"Sure. After the break."

"I've got a tape of it," he says.

Regulars demand familiarity. They all have several songs they expect to hear each night. I sing them, knowing I'm repeating their stories; let the words evoke characters from my past—an unrequited love, perhaps, or one that spent itself.

Spent. Like passion. Or a paycheque. Not much difference. Both leave you hungry.

"That song reminds me of someone," Dave says. "Could have been written for me."

"Listen, Dave," I say. "Lenny here's just come into town. Haven't seen him for a while. You don't mind, do you?" I don't want to hear the story of his life, though he's sure to tell me at some point during this week.

"No problem." He slides off the bar stool slowly. "I'll catch you later."

"Thanks for the drink," Lenny says.

I sip my scotch slowly, resisting the tug of familiarity. Slipping back into that blurred screen.

"You living in the same place?" Lenny asks.

"Yeah."

"Alone?"

"No."

We each stare into our glasses.

"I quit drinking," he says.

"So what's that in front of you?"

"Regular drinking, I mean."

And I'm reading between the lines. "How's Anne?" I ask.

"We split up six months ago," he says.

"You or her?"

"She moved out while I was on the road."

I curb an insane urge to laugh. Swallow instead. "Yeah?"

"She'd been carrying on with the guy for the past year. Never told me."

"And you always did, I suppose."

We are silent again. Untold words hang between us. I sigh, and look at my watch.

"I'm on," I say. "You leaving or staying?"

"I'll stay."

I head for the other side of the piano. Begin playing. Trying not to remember my history with men. An ongoing montage. Emotional wastelands. Variations. But I'm thinking of Gary and Lenny. And it's like switching reels and I'm in another B-grade movie. This time, the woman must choose between two men: the responsible, down-to-earth variety and the reckless rogue. One offers a lifetime of boredom; the other a lifetime of hassles. So I think to myself, wait a minute. These are neither/nors.

Imagine the scene: split-screen: in the top half, luxurious living-room. The central image, a telephone. Partial view of a man pacing the room. Several times, he walks to the phone as if to pick it up, then changes his mind. In the lower half, sleazy hotel room, another man, another telephone. Duplicates. Screen #1 or Screen #2?

In the movie, the woman always chooses the concrete, the guarantee. Protection and safety. (Risks don't happen in black & white.) Violins soar in her moment of epiphany: *she actually loves him.* What a silly fool she's been. Quick. Call up the top screen. "What a silly fool I've been," she says. THE END. Woman saved once again by virtuous man. The violin section swells in major chords. Bust a string, would you?

I sing the last three songs. Turn off the amps, and slide off the piano stool. Then, I begin to slowly unplug my patch chords. Wrap them in circles between my elbow and hand, carefully unwinding all the kinks. I secure each tidy coil with gaffer tape, then hurl it into my case and slam the lid shut.

"You want to go for a bite to eat?" Lenny asks.

"I've got to go. It's late."

"You wearing a watch now?" he says.

"It's no good," I say.

"I guess I should have done this a long time ago, huh?"

I shrug, and begin putting on my jacket.

He lays his hand on my arm. "This guy you're with. Is it serious?"

"Not any more," I tell him.

"Wait a minute," he says. "You got a pen?"

I search through my purse for one. He scribbles his phone number on the inside of a matchbook.

"Call me sometime?"

"Sure," I say, though I know I won't.

So I step out. Which brings me to number three. Wavy screen. And suddenly, I'm in the cool night air, in full colour. I get into my car, start up the motor, thinking white steed galloping. And in this movie, the woman rides into a dawn sky, to a musical score of banjos and flutes. Or perhaps to a rousing chorus of gospel harmonies. Good spell. She has a smile on her face, and the wind machine blows the hair away from her forehead. The credits roll. And she rides, determined, into the unknown.